Brody's Back

Other books in the series

Starring Sammie

Starring Brody

Starring Alex

Starring Jolene

Sammie's Back

Alex's Back

Jolene's Back

Brody's Back

—the girl who's got it all (well, that's what everyone else thinks)

Helena Pielichaty

Illustrated by Melanie Williamson

OXFORD
UNIVERSITY PRESS

OXFORD
UNIVERSITY PRESS
Great Clarendon Street, Oxford OX2 6DP

Oxford University Press is a department of the University of Oxford.
It furthers the University's objective of excellence in research, scholarship,
and education by publishing worldwide in

Oxford New York

Auckland Cape Town Dar es Salaam Hong Kong Karachi
Kuala Lumpur Madrid Melbourne Mexico City Nairobi
New Delhi Shanghai Taipei Toronto

With offices in

Argentina Austria Brazil Chile Czech Republic France Greece
Guatemala Hungary Italy Japan Poland Portugal Singapore
South Korea Switzerland Thailand Turkey Ukraine Vietnam

Oxford is a registered trade mark of Oxford University Press
in the UK and in certain other countries

British Library Cataloguing in Publication Data

Data available

ISBN-13: 978-0-19-275378-6
ISBN-10: 0-19-275378-9

1 3 5 7 9 10 8 6 4 2

Typset by Palimpsest Book Production Limited,
Polmont, Stirlingshire

Printed in Great Britain by Cox and Wyman Ltd., Reading, Berkshire

for Zuzia
with special thanks to all those involved in
the North Wales Book Quiz for inspiring
the Big Book Quiz in this story

Chapter One

The guy at the door asked if Mom was home. He was fiftyish and round-bellied with the shiniest, baldest head I had ever seen. He seemed to be struggling with the flat parcel in his hands as much as I was with the school tie in mine. 'Well, she is home,' I began, trying to loop the contrary tie the school-rule way, which is complicated without a mirror or a diploma in origami, 'but I've gotta warn you eight o'clock in the morning is not a great time to call, unless someone died. Did someone die?' I glanced up at him and grinned, to show I was kidding—about the dying part anyhow.

'Er . . . not that I know of,' the guy replied solemnly.

I sighed and began to explain. 'See, we both slept through the alarm, which means I missed my bus, so Mom now has to take me to school and you know what that one-way system is like this time on Mondays. I'll probably end up on detention . . . they're really keen on punctuality at Queen Mary's . . . that's the school I go to. Do you know the one I mean? It's a real old building near the art gallery and the hospital . . . though only some of it's old; there are some new bits.'

The guy furrowed his eyebrows, as if he had a headache coming on. Boy, his head was shiny. Did he polish it every night? 'Well, anyway,' I rattled on, 'I've had three lateness warnings already this term; my form tutor, Mrs Hanson, calls me tardy. It isn't a compliment but isn't that just the coolest word ever? Tardy?'

'Erm . . .' the guy said, adjusting the parcel and looking uncomfortable. I guess maybe I had over-loaded him with too much information; I like to share. There was a sudden shriek from Mom somewhere behind me as the phone began ringing.

'Could you come back at four? Four would be better, believe me,' I told him, 'Mom's usually caught up with everything by then. Oh, but not today. Mondays, she's at the gym till six.'

The guy frowned. 'Look, love, I'm only 'ere now because your cleaner told me this was the best time to catch the house owner in.'

I nodded. 'Well, she's right, normally it would be, but not *this* morning,' I told him, 'maybe I can take a message instead?'

He shook his head. 'I don't have a message,' he said, 'I just have aerial photographs . . . you know . . . to sell. The one of your house . . .' His eyes darted to the lettering chiselled in the sandstone architrave '. . . Kirkham Lodge . . . is a beaut. Look.'

He pulled back the brown paper wrapping to show me. There it was, home sweet home

3

in full bird's-eye view and glorious technicolour; not only the house but also the orchard, the stable block, the swimming pool, the outbuildings, the drive, the walled garden; even the hidden den where I used to hang out. 'What do you think?' the guy asked, 'only thirty-nine ninety-nine including the gilt frame and non-reflective glass—bargain.'

'I think,' I said, finally managing to loop my tie into some kind of knot, 'I think you'd better come in,' and I called for Mom.

In the entrance hall, Mom held the gilt-framed picture like a tea-tray ready to beat someone over the head with and shot the guy a ferocious look. 'What is this again?' she asked in disbelief, the sleeves of her silk kimono fanning out over the torn packaging.

The guy gave her the spiel about the gilt frame and the non-reflective glass. She was not impressed. 'You mean you're telling me this is legal? That it's perfectly OK for strangers just to go round taking pictures of people's property without permission? From a helicopter?'

He blanched at Mom's acid tone and began

stammering an explanation. 'Well . . . I don't know . . . I've only just started, like, but the firm's legit . . . got awards and all sorts.'

'Show me some ID, bud!' Mom suddenly demanded, leaning the picture against the wall and holding out her hand. He quickly pulled a bent laminated card from the breast pocket of his shirt. 'G. K. Vistas of West Yorkshire. Huh!' Mom snapped, returning it to him.

The salesman began to look nervous. 'You don't have to buy the picture, love, there's no obligation. If you don't want a unique perspective of your home, Mrs . . . ?'

'Miller!' Mom snapped giving the poor guy a frosty 'as-if-you-didn't-know' look.

'Mrs Miller . . . that's your right. I'll just take it back and . . .'

'Oh, I don't think so, buster!' Mom stormed, seizing the frame before turning on her heels and hurrying barefoot down the hallway to fetch her purse.

He stared after her, seeming puzzled that he'd actually got a sale. 'Don't take it personally; it's a privacy thing,' I said to him when she was out of earshot. 'We get a lot of paparazzi round trying to take unsolicited photos of us. You know—ex-model with no make-up on shock-horror. My dad was in court only last week for punching a photographer who gate-crashed our Christmas party.'

The salesman's face cleared suddenly, as if the penny had dropped. 'Your dad's Jake Miller? The photographer?'

'Yep.'

'Well, I never! I remember reading about that! I can see where your mum's coming from now.'

'I thought you might.'

I was desperate to touch his shiny head, just to see what it felt like, but I managed to resist and just said 'so long' once Mom had returned and paid him.

In the kitchen I found Orla, our cleaner, staring at the aerial photograph which was now propped against the garbage bin. 'Yer mammy wants me to throw it away,' she said in her awesome Irish accent. 'It seems a shame, especially after paying all that for it.' Orla hates being wasteful, especially when it comes to money.

I quickly peeled the lid off a raspberry yoghurt pot. 'It's not our kind of thing,' I explained.

Orla shook her can of starch vigorously before blasting it at one of my school shirts ready for ironing, her bare, freckly arms moving rapidly back and forth across the ironing board. 'Really? I think it's grand; it shows every detail.'

'That's the problem.'

Orla looked confused, as she often does at our 'ways' as she calls them, but I didn't have time to explain. 'Brody!' Mom yelled from the hallway. 'Pick up the pace; let's go.'

'Coming!' I reached for my school bag, which was heavy enough to make a Marine wince, so I knew I had everything packed for

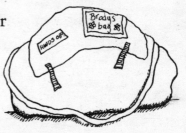

QM's. Something was nagging me, though, and I glanced round the kitchen for inspiration.

'Forgotten something?' Orla asked. 'Our Robert's the same. He'd forget his head if it were loose. Take last night . . .'

I knew if I stopped to listen to one of Orla's

anecdotes about her nineteen-year-old 'fickless' son I wouldn't get to school until lunchtime, intriguing though they were, so I just smiled apologetically and made for the door. 'Gotta go, Orla, or Mrs Hanson will blow a fuse. See you.'

She sprayed the same shirtsleeve again. 'Just you tell her the good is never late, darlin'.'

'I will!'

Chapter Two

Believe it or not, my mom managed to get me across town and screech to a halt outside the entrance to Queen Mary's with three whole minutes to spare. I don't know why I was so surprised we'd made it; Mom used to drive across New York, so central Wakefield is small cheese in comparison. I guess her total disregard for speed humps and give-way signs helped a little, too. She parked on the double yellow lines and I leaned across to kiss her goodbye. 'See you tonight after club, hon,' she smiled.

By that she means the After School club at my

old primary school, Zetland Avenue. It's like a cross between a youth club and a crèche for kids who want to stay on to do activities out of school hours. I had been worried I wouldn't be able to continue going once I started secondary school because it was the only place I could hang out with Reggie, my boyfriend. During summer, though, Mrs Fryston, the supervisor of the club, on another of her recruitment drives, raised the upper age limit from eleven to thirteen. *Et voilà*— problem solved!

'OK, Kiersten, drive safe now,' I told my mom as I turned to follow the few other stragglers indoors.

'I will—oh, and good luck with your book quiz practice,' she called.

I twisted back round, my hand over my mouth. That's what had been bugging me in the kitchen! 'Doh!'

Mom peered over the rim of her sunglasses at me. 'Brody! You didn't forget the books?'

I nodded. Mrs Fryston had organized this thing called the Big Book Quiz against other clubs in

the district and I had somehow ended up as captain of the team. Fine example I was setting, forgetting the actual books we were being quizzed on in the 'Fantastic Classics' section. I was meant to pass them on to Lloyd Fountain, one of my team-mates, today in time for the first round on Thursday. Eek!

Kiersten leaned out of the window and called after me. 'You're going to have to get better organized, young lady.'

'I know, I know!' I yelled back as the buzzer sounded from inside the main entrance and I headed up the path, 'I know!'

I never used to be disorganized at all; it's just that everything is a bit harder since I began high school. Don't get me wrong; I like life at Queen Mary's. Nearly all the teachers are human beings and I've made heaps of new friends but there's so much more to take on board than there was at primary school. We start earlier and finish later and the school's further away which eats into both ends of my day. Plus there are all the extra-curricula activities that go on around it, like basketball and flute and drama, not to mention the stacks of rules and even more stacks of homework. Then there are my visits to the orthodontist's in between to fix the veneer on my front tooth. I lost the original tooth months ago—long story, don't ask—but because I'm still growing my mouth shape keeps changing so I have to have regular check-ups to keep an eye on everything. I just thank Dixie I don't model for Jake any more or I'd have to get Mom to bid for sleep for me on e-Bay. All in all, ZAPS After School club is kind of low on my list these days, which is why I didn't think twice about the books *again* until Reggie mentioned them after school.

Reggie always meets me after school. The

Magna, where he goes, finishes earlier than Queen Mary's so he walks across town to wait for me and we catch the bus to ZAPS together. All together now—awww!

'Hey up, Hairy Mary,' he greeted me, as usual.

'Hi there, Magna Boy,' I returned.

Awwwww!

'Have you got those books for Lloyd?' he asked before I'd even got out of the gateway. 'Only you told me to remind you as soon as I saw you.'

'Nope,' I replied, pulling off my tie and pushing it as far down into my bag as it would go before falling into step next to him. I say next to: I had this growth spurt during the summer and shot up to five-six but Reggie kind of stayed the same, so really I ought to walk on the road and keep him on the pavement if we want to stay level. Not that height's an issue or anything.

Reggie just shrugged. 'Well, I kept my side of the bargain,' he said and reached out for my hand.

'I forgot the books. I was tardy again this morning,' I confessed.

'You want to get yourself a better alarm clock, woman,' Reggie admonished, 'or a better memory.'

'Yeah, yeah, yeah.'

'Yeah, yeah, yeah,' Reggie repeated.

We crossed over the road by the art gallery and headed into the centre of town, chatting so intently about lessons and homework and teachers we almost missed the Zetland Avenue bus. 'I'll help you with your French if you help me with my maths when we get to After School club,' I told Reggie as we flopped down on the seat. He is chronic at French and I am chronic at maths so it's a fair trade. There's a special home-work area at the club, known as Boff Corner, where we work, and sometimes, if no one's looking, hold hands.

He grunted though. 'Fine, if Ruby lets us. She was in a well crabby mood this morning.'

'Oh yeah,' I agreed, rolling my eyes in sympathy, 'Ruby.'

Chapter Three

Ruby is Reggie's little sister. She only started at After School club in January and isn't even five yet, but she is definitely high maintenance. As if to demonstrate, as soon as we arrived in the mobile, the 'temporary' portakabin on the edge of the school playground where After School club meets, she flew towards Reggie and head-butted him right in the nuts before he had a chance to dodge. 'You're late, Reg! The big hand on the clock's way after the twelve!' she declared, brushing her long dark fringe out of her eyes.

'Get lost, you maniac!' Reggie protested, doubling over in agony.

'No!' she said, and set her head down again like a ram about to . . . well, ram, I guess. Whether it was just plain coincidence, or Mrs Fryston did actually have mind-reading skills as I have long suspected, she chose that precise moment to come over to us. 'Hello, you two,' she greeted Reggie and me while placing her hands lightly on Ruby's shoulders, stopping her in her tracks, 'how was school?'

'Fine,' we chorused.

'Mine wasn't!' Ruby declared. 'I had to eat fruit! I hate fruit!'

'Well, why don't you come and help me with the refreshment tray? I'm sure we can find something healthy but non-fruity for you,' Mrs Fryston suggested.

'OK,' Ruby agreed affably enough, giving Reggie and me the all-clear to head for Boff Corner. Just as I began to follow Reggie, though, Mrs Fryston tapped me lightly. 'Brody, can I ask you a favour?' she smiled sweetly.

'Sure,' I said.

'I was in the middle of a game of Jenga with that little group over there. Would you mind taking my place while I help Ruby?'

'Er . . . no,' I said. One good turn deserves another, I guess.

The game didn't take long and I was just about to try to join Reggie over in Boff Corner when Mrs Fryston clapped her hands together. 'OK, everyone, time for our run-through of the book quiz,' she announced brightly. 'As we're the hosts for the first round on Thursday, we need to practise where we're going to sit and what we're going to do when the other teams arrive. Ruby is going to show us how it's done.'

Demurely, Princess Ruby walked to the centre of the carpeted area and sat down. Mrs Fryston congratulated her and turned away, thereby missing the hefty push Ruby gave to Brandon a

second later when he attempted to sit beside her.
'That space is for Reggie!' she hissed.

Reggie sighed and sat beside her, knowing he wouldn't have any peace unless he obeyed. I joined him, to give moral support. Even now, Ruby had begun pinching Reggie's arm and he had to swat her hand away to stop her, the little poppet.

Mrs Fryston, a sheaf of papers in her hand, nodded in satisfaction at the assembled group. 'Lovely,' she beamed, 'there should be more than enough space for everyone on the day. The adult helpers from the other After School clubs will sit round the sides and they're only bringing their actual teams with them, who will all be at tables up here.' She indicated the row of empty dining tables borrowed from the main school next to her. 'Now, could the quiz team members come out to the front, please?'

'You should have volunteered,' I whispered to Reggie as I rose to my feet. 'You could have escaped Nipper Noreen then.'

'Told you, book quizzes are gay,' he said,

rubbing his arm. 'And I'm not like you. I can say no when people ask favours,' he added.

I ignored this sad but true fact about me and went to join my team-mates.

'Hi, gang,' I beamed.

Lloyd Fountain, Alex McCormack, and Sam Riley smiled at me and returned my high-fives. I quickly apologized to Lloyd for forgetting the books. 'Got distracted by a bald guy selling aerial photographs,' I told him. 'It's a long story,' I added when he looked at me a little confused.

Lloyd gave me half a smile, said it didn't matter, he'd read them all anyway—twice.

'I knew you would have,' I fibbed, sighing with relief. I then turned to Mrs Fryston, 'OK, ma'am, bring it on.'

Chapter Four

That was kind of it, really; a day in the life of Brody Miller. Kiersten picked me up about six, just as the rehearsal ended, and chatted with some of the other carers while I finished 'bigging up' my team and reassuring Mrs Fryston Thursday would rock. 'The sample questions weren't too hard?' she probed.

'Nope.'

'Or too easy?'

'Nope.'

She smiled. 'Good. There's just the decor to sort out then. I was thinking a few posters dotted round the place and maybe some streamers. What do you think?'

'Go for it,' I said.

Her eyes twinkled. 'I think we should. Can I borrow you tomorrow to help? You're so lovely and tall.'

There goes my time in Boff Corner with Reggie, I thought, but how could I refuse? 'Sure,' I said.

In the car, Kiersten asked me how my day had been, and then, as usual, I asked her about hers. We got home, I changed into my comfortable clothes, had dinner, talked to Jake on the phone in London about how many models had thrown a hissy fit during his shoot that day, did some homework, watched a little TV, practised my flute for a half hour, e-mailed Reggie and then went to bed. Pretty regular stuff, huh? Nothing for the paparazzi to get excited about there.

The next day started out much the same, except I managed to get up in time and no salesmen with dodgy pictures called round. The first change came when Reggie wouldn't go into the mobile, refusing to climb the steps like a horse pulling up at a difficult fence. 'Suss out where the Rube is first,' he directed and made me peer through the glass in the door. It didn't take long to locate her; I just focused on the area from where the most movement was coming.

I relayed my findings like a TV reporter. 'Er . . . you join us now as Miss Glazzard, wearing a fetching scowl, appears to be fighting with Master Brandon Petty over the infamous red cowboy boots in the dressing-up box. Miss Glazzard seems to be winning the fight. Yep, she's got the left boot on her right foot now and she's going for the right on her left. Oh, wait, there's been a comeback. Master Petty, who has won this fight on three previous occasions, is not giving in . . . he's tugging away, despite frenetic kicking actions from Glazzard and . . . oh, shame . . . here comes the referee, Fearless Fryston, to separate them. But oh, no, Miss Glazzard is not accepting the referee's decision and she's thrown the boot clear across the arena where it has landed on . . . Mucky Mick the hamster's cage . . . There's uproar from the animal rights movement who are all protesting about the foul throw . . .'

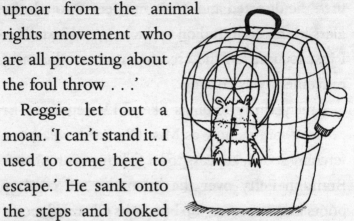

Reggie let out a moan. 'I can't stand it. I used to come here to escape.' He sank onto the steps and looked miserably at the tarmac. I sat down next to him.

'I know; it's not the same now, is it?'

'You can say that again.'

'I mean, I knew it would be different this year with us both being at secondary school and older than everyone else but I didn't know it would be different because you've got a nutso sister.'

'Not forgetting the nutso brother when I get home.'

For the record, Reggie meant Ben, who is

seventeen. He sounded just like Orla's Robert and Sammie's older sister Gemma, always in one scrape or another. 'What's he done now?' I asked.

'What? Apart from writing Dad's car off last week and getting engaged without telling anyone and chucking up college to go backpacking? Nothing much.'

'Oops.'

My boyfriend pulled the lids of his eyes down over his eyeballs. Gross. 'To zink I am ze normal one of zee family,' he said in a voice meant to sound like Dr Frankenstein.

'Go figure.'

'Mum says if it wasn't for me she'd crack up.'

'I'm so glad I'm an only child,' I laughed and leaned my head against Reggie's shoulder. It would have been a nice moment, apart from the cold wind whipping at my face and the empty crisp packets blowing round our feet and the relentless thudding coming from the side of the mobile. 'What's that?' I asked, sitting up.

'Dunno; probably Ruby thumping somebody,' Reggie said.

I glanced along the side of the mobile, where the door to the equipment shed, a windowless lean-to wooden extension tagged on the side of the mobile hut, was banging to and fro. 'Reggie,' I said, getting up slowly and pulling him with me, 'I think I've found a solution to our problem.'

Chapter Five

We sneaked into the shed. 'This is cosy!' I said, sinking onto a pile of beanbags in the corner.

'Yeah,' Reggie agreed, flopping next to me, 'and quiet.'

'A Ruby-free zone.'

'Exactly.'

'You wait here and I'll go sign us in,' I told him but as I got up, a gust of wind caught the shed door, sending it banging shut and plunging us into darkness.

'Oh!' I said, groping for Reggie's hand.

'What's up? You're not scared are you?' he asked.

'As if! I love the dark; I was just taken by surprise. Why? Are you?' I replied sitting back down again.

'Petrified,' he said in a hushed voice.

We sat for ages, just holding hands and not speaking. I don't know why. I mean, normally we don't shut up but it was as if the shed expected silence. The air grew warm around us and I felt so cosy. I knew we should go and sign in but time seemed to stand still somehow.

'Hey, Reggie,' I whispered.

'What?' he whispered back.

'Now that it's too dark to do anything else do you think we could . . .'

'What?' Reggie asked worriedly.

I felt shy all of a sudden. 'Do this,' I said quickly and kissed him on the lips!

He didn't say anything at first. 'What do you think?' I prompted, feeling all floaty.

'It was all right,' Reggie said.

'Only "all right"?'

'Well, you took me by surprise.'

'Huh! OK. Reggie, when I count to three, I'm

going to kiss you movie-style. One . . . two . . .'

'Three!' Reggie said, beating me to it by kissing me first this time. 'Yep,' he said afterwards, 'definitely all right.'

Nobody really noticed we were late; Mrs Fryston was still giving Ruby a lesson in 'sharing' and Sammie's dad Mr Wesley, who worked as one of the assistants now, was trying to right the bars of Mucky Mick's cage and everyone else was just getting on with things. Reggie and I ambled casually, but separately, across to Boff Corner where Lloyd asked me to test him on *The Lion, the Witch and the Wardrobe* because he felt he didn't know it well enough for Thursday. 'Sure,' I said, my voice coming out a little higher and lighter than normal.

A few minutes later Mrs Fryston sent Alex over for me to help with the decorating. 'What decorating?' Reggie asked.

'For the Book Quiz,' I told him, only just remembering myself. 'Wanna help?'

He stared at the posters Alex was carrying and shook his head. 'No,' he said flatly. I was beginning to wish I'd said no, too. I'd have much preferred to sit next to Reggie, but a deal's a deal.

I don't know where she'd got them from but Mrs Fryston had enough posters of books to wallpaper Buckingham Palace. It seemed to take for ever to mount them. I guess it would have taken less time if my eyes hadn't kept sliding across to Reggie. He did his best to ignore me but I knew, from the way the tips of his ears turned pink when he did look across, that his stomach was as knotted up as mine. Swapping kisses was definitely better than swapping homework. We'd be checking out that hut again for sure.

Chapter Six

Next day we scurried straight in there. 'We have to get this kissing lark sorted in private first, or we'll never be able to show them in public,' Reggie had reasoned on the bus.

I had agreed with him totally and we wasted no time in starting rehearsals. 'Just one more then we'll go in,' I murmured after the first few. 'I've got to prep my team for tomorrow and Mrs Fryston wants even more decorating doing. She's really going over-the-top with this quiz lark.'

'Whatever,' Reggie agreed, then leapt up as if he'd been shot.

'What's the matter?' I asked him in alarm.

'I heard voices.'

'So?'

'Mothers' voices!'

'I heard music,' I sighed.

Reggie wasn't listening. He was already feeling his way towards the door when it was opened from the outside. The sudden light made me blink. 'Oh!' Mr Wesley said, almost dropping the rolled-up play mat in his arms. A look of relief crossed his face. 'We've been wondering where you two had got to.' He levered the play mat into the corner and called out over his shoulder, 'It's all right, he's out here, Mrs Glazzard.'

There was a clattering sound as Reggie's mum charged down the mobile steps in the high, clicky heels she always wore to make her seem taller, and appeared at the door, a worried look on her face. 'Reggie, pet! I've been in a panic! What are you doing in here?'

'Nothing,' Reggie mumbled, his head bowed as he stepped out into the daylight. I could see he was blushing hard: the tips of his ears were bright,

bright pink. 'Anyway, what are *you* doing *here*? It's not even half four yet.'

Mrs Glazzard crushed her son to her chest and gave him a huge peck on his forehead. 'Can't a mother come early to see the light of her life?'

'Mum! Pack it in with the sloppy stuff, will you! I've got my public to consider.'

'Public? What public?'

'I think he means me,' I laughed, stepping out of the shed as well. 'Hi, Mrs Glazzard.'

Mrs Glazzard turned and looked at me in surprise; I don't think she had realized I had been inside the hut, too. Her eyes flicked over to me, over Reggie, then into the hut. I felt like a fly caught on a show cake when it was about to be judged.

'Well!' she said finally. 'This is a fine example, I must say.'

I was still feeling floaty from the movie-kisses and just smiled, not really understanding what she meant. I found out later, though. Oh boy, did I.

Chapter Seven

The first clue that something was wrong was when there was no Reggie waiting for me the next day after school. I waited outside school for ages and ages, missing my usual bus from town, just in case he arrived at the last minute, which was not the smartest thing to do when you were supposed to be taking part in a book quiz.

Even when I remembered about it, I didn't hurry from the bus stop to the club; my mind was still more on Reggie than 'Fantastic Classics'. It wasn't until I reached the mobile and discovered that it was totally empty, I got a jolt. I hadn't got the dates wrong, had I? It wasn't the weekend or anything?

A sign directing people to the school hall confused me even more. Why were we in there? Especially when we'd spent all that time jazzing up the mobile with posters and streamers? I sloped across to the main school building, wondering about the amount of noise coming from the hall. Sammie grabbed my arm as soon as I entered. 'Oh! Brody! It's a good job you've arrived! I think Mrs Fryston's nearly having a nervous breakdown.'

'What's going on?' I asked, surveying the dozens and dozens of kids sitting in clusters on the parquet flooring. 'I thought we were just having the actual teams and a helper per club?'

Sammie nodded in agreement. 'We were meant to! Trouble is they've *all* come with *all* their kids— like it's the final or something—so we had to ask Mr Sharkey if we could use the hall and luckily he was taking part anyway so he said yes but Mrs Bailey's not right chuffed because she was halfway through her buffing . . .'

I glanced across to where Mrs Bailey, the

caretaker, was standing redundantly at the edge of the hall, leaning against her immobilized polisher. Across from her, Mrs Fryston, waving her hand frantically for me to come to the front.

'Oh, well, here goes,' I said leaving my bag with Sammie.

'Good luck.'

'Thanks,' I said, thinking I'd need it.

Chairs had been stacked against steamed-up windows and tables piled haphazardly down the sides of the hall. At random intervals, bored-looking adults in various coloured sweatshirts sat with arms folded, waiting for kick-off. There wasn't room for me to sidle my way inconspicuously to the ZAPS table so I had to pick my way through the crowds of after-school-clubbers. It all felt like a disastrous kid's birthday party where the magician hadn't appeared. No wonder Mrs Fryston seemed frazzled.

She was standing at the front, a too-wide smile planted on her face. 'Thank goodness you're here, Brody,' she said, clasping me on the shoulder when I reached her.

'Have you been waiting just for me?' I asked in horror. 'You should have just started without me.'

'No, it's not your fault if people can't read letters giving clear instructions about times and numbers,' she muttered. She then took a deep breath, then puffed out her cheeks to release some tension. 'Anyway, they would have refused,' she said, a little more lightly, indicating my team whose table was directly behind. Alex and Sam gave me a relieved 'thumbs-up' but Lloyd stared blankly beyond me, his face pale and anxious.

'What's wrong with Lloyd?' I whispered.

'He's a little overwhelmed, I think; he's never been in anything like this before,' Mrs Fryston whispered back. 'I was hoping you could help him; pass on some of your boundless confidence.'

'Sure,' I said and switched straight into Brody the Reliable mode.

Lloyd was home-schooled; it figured he

wouldn't have done much in front of an audience before, like assemblies and school plays. Taking the only empty team seat, I grinned at them all but kept eye contact with Lloyd. 'Lloyd Fountain,' I said in a serious tone, 'for two points, what does the S in C. S. Lewis stand for?'

'Staples,' he replied instantly in a low voice.

'And that's what you'll get on your butt if you don't answer every question right.'

He smiled, a little wonkily, but he smiled all the same.

'OK, team, let's party!' I said.

Chapter Eight

Mrs Fryston now stepped forward and indicated she was ready by clapping her hands and smiling widely at her audience. There was some shuffling, a lot of hushing from various adults and the manoeuvring of the more challenging little individuals to sit within arm's length. Ruby was one of them. I glimpsed her being plucked out of her row by Mrs McCormack and placed firmly on her lap. So if Ruby Dooby Do was here, where was Reggie? Sick? Never mind, I told myself sternly. Better focus.

'Well, isn't this fantastic?' Mrs Fryston boomed,

wasting no time in introducing Mr Sharkey as the Quizmaster. I should have guessed my old head teacher couldn't resist taking part; he loved anything book related. Plus, he'd donate a kidney to help Mrs Fryston out; they were so in 'lurve'. Did you know they were getting married in May. How cool is that?

Anyway, Mr Sharkey stepped out from behind the dressing-up screen wearing the shiny silk waistcoat he always used to don for special occasions, stroked his beard and grinned at us all. 'Right then, boys and girls, let's see who knows their books! The first ten questions will be about one of my favourites, *The Turbulent Term of Tyke Tyler* by Gene Kemp. Wrenthorpe After Schoolers, for one easy-peasy point, who wrote . . .'

So the opening round of the Big Book Quiz kicked off. As it was a team round and we could confer, Lloyd's quiet responses went unnoticed. He knew his stuff, though, and I kept whispering things to him like, 'You go, buster,' when he won us a point. Most of the questions were similar to the ones Mrs Fryston had rehearsed with us on

Monday so it was all pretty straightforward 'name the main character' kind of stuff.

I guess other play leaders had done the same because by the end all the teams were pretty balanced apart from a couple of clubs who obviously hadn't a clue. The team directly next to us, the Tea-Time Tigers, for instance, consisting of three girls and a sour-faced boy with his arm in a cast, didn't seem to know zip.

Just for the record, this round wasn't too crucial. The idea was that all the teams' points were carried forward to round two, Pick a Peck of Poets. It was after *that* when the big boys came out to play. Only four teams qualified for the Grand Finale in the Wakefield Drury Lane Library on World Book Day. Whether ZAPS would be one of them was anyone's guess but we had to be in with a chance.

At the end, a young woman with crimson spiky hair and a Simple Minds T-shirt, stalked up to Mrs Fryston. 'How old did you say the children had to be to take part?' she demanded, looking straight at me when she said it.

Mrs Fryston seemed taken aback by her tone. 'Well, I didn't mention an upper age limit, but as thirteen is the cut-off age, then I suppose it's thirteen. The main criterion is they have to attend an After School club . . .'

'Well,' the supervisor said, firing another shot at my uniform, 'I wish I'd known earlier.'

'Who was that?' I asked afterwards as I helped stack chairs.

'That was Ms Spilsby, the Tea-Time Tigers' supervisor.'

'Well, she's got an attitude problem.'

'Yes,' Mrs Fryston agreed, staring into the distance, 'just a little.'

Chapter Nine

'Gee, I mean, it's not as if I was the brainiac of the team; Lloyd was that!' I fumed as I told Mom all about the quiz and Ms Spilsby at the end.

Mom laughed. 'Well, when you're taller people do think you're older than everyone else,' she said, slowing to pull into our driveway. 'I had that all my life, too.'

'People shouldn't jump to conclusions.'

'Oh, it has its advantages. I got to see a whole bunch of films I wasn't supposed to!'

'Huh! That's only OK if you're with someone

43

else tall. What would I do with Reggie? Make him wait outside the movies?'

Mom pulled over in front of the garage and got this dumb, slushy look on her face. 'Aw. You and Reggie. It's so sweet! Have you had your first kiss yet?'

Too close to home, lady! I could feel my face burning. 'Mom! Shut up!'

She jumped down from the car and winked at me. 'I'll take that as a "yes" then. Oh, my baby's had her first kiss! I wonder what time it is in Topeka so I can call your grandma and tell her.'

'Kiersten! Don't you dare!'

'Brody and Reggie sitting in a tree, k-i-s-s-i-n-g . . .' Mom chanted, as she headed towards the house. So mature.

'You weren't serious about calling Topeka, were you?' I asked, dumping my bag on the worktop Orla had done a neat job of polishing.

'Well, maybe after dinner,' she said, followed by another wink.

'Good, 'cause I need to call Reggie first—in private.'

'Give him a kiss from me,' she teased. Honestly.

I headed for the living room and dialled Reggie's number; I had so much to tell him. Mrs Glazzard answered. 'Hi, Mrs Glazzard, it's Brody. Is Reggie there, please?' There was a long pause.

'Mrs Glazzard?'

'No, Brody, Reggie's not here.'

'Oh, OK, I'll call back later.'

'No!' she said sharply.

'Excuse me?'

'Please do *not* call back later. In fact, I'd appreciate it if you did not call back at all.'

'Is something wrong, ma'am?'

'Yes! Yes! Something is wrong "ma'am". Something's been wrong since you decided to play boyfriend and girlfriend at this ridiculously silly age with my son. What on earth did you think you were up to in that hut?'

'Erm . . .'

'"Erm" indeed! Well, it's stopping right now, Brody. Reggie will not be meeting you after school any more, he will not be spending hours on the phone with you in the evenings, and, until he apologizes for being extremely rude to me yesterday, he will not be returning to After School club! I've already got one idiot of a son where girls are concerned, I'm not having you turn Reggie into another!'

'But, Mrs Glazzard, I . . .'

'Please do not argue with me! I know you've been brought up differently from other children your age, which is why you behave a lot older than you actually are, and I expect you're used to having your own way, but not this time, all right?'

'But, Mrs Glazzard . . .'

'Not this time! End of conversation, Brody.'

It was too. All I could hear was the buzzing of the line as it went dead.

Chapter Ten

Wow! I don't think Miss Hogenboom, my English teacher, would approve but 'gobsmacked' is the nearest word I can think of to describe how I felt after that phone call. My mouth was certainly the most affected. The rest of me I could get to work OK; my arms and my legs and all my other bits did their usual thing. My mouth was totally not functioning. It had been gobsmacked into not working properly. It couldn't tell Mom why I couldn't eat dinner that night and it couldn't say hello back when Orla greeted me the next morning and it couldn't smile when Mrs Fryston congratulated the team, and especially my leadership during the book quiz, at After School club Friday tea-time.

By Sunday evening, and not one e-mail or phone call from Reggie, I began wondering what I'd do if he never came to After School club again. Reggie was the only reason I still went—there was no point otherwise. I know I sound pathetic and girlie and lame but I don't care. Reggie was my best friend. I felt lopsided without him. And let's face it, I did look out of place there. I towered above every kid who attended. Heck, I was almost level with Mrs Fryston and even she treated me more like an assistant than an attendee these days.

I sighed, slid off the bed and mooched across to my windowsill where I gazed at my collection of snow globes. I love my snow globes. Some people like to cuddle up with stuffed toys or blankets when they're fed up but I preferred the smooth, cold feel of the rounded glass in my palm. I like shaking the snow particles about until they settle, then shaking again. That comforts me somehow. I had fifteen of them, mostly presents from my relatives in the States, all in a row. The one of the Statue of Liberty was my favourite and I reached out for it now.

'What am I going to do, Lib?' I asked out loud as the glitter whirled round her outstretched arm.

'Sort it out, puppy dog, your mooning's making me hurl,' she told me sternly.

'Right,' I replied, 'I will.'

Chapter Eleven

This is what I did. My last lesson on a Monday is history with Mr Carpenter but instead of heading towards room sixteen, I turned in the opposite direction and dodged into the girls' cloakroom. When everything in the corridor fell silent, I began to walk towards the main exit. Of course, who should be coming straight towards me but Mrs Hanson! My hand automatically shot to my mouth as I cursed myself for being caught bunking off so soon. 'Hello, Brody. Where are you going?' Mrs Hanson asked immediately.

I could only manage a few stutters, I was so nervous. 'I . . . my . . .'

'Is it your tooth?' she asked. My tooth? Of course! I hadn't taken my hand away from my mouth and she'd seen enough orthodontist appointment cards from me to jump to the wrong conclusion.

I nodded, 'It's . . . it's come loose . . . it feels gross. Mom's . . . Mom's picking me up to take me straight to the orthodontist's.' Jeez, I didn't realize I was so good at lying; Mrs Hanson looked at me with real concern.

'I'm sorry. Do you want me to wait with you?'

I shook my head, keeping my hand firmly in front of my troublesome mouth.

'Well, if you're sure?'

I nodded again and she wished me good luck and headed towards the staffroom.

I used the same excuse at Reception, seeing as it appeared to be so convincing. 'Oh, you poor thing,' the receptionist said as I went to sign out. 'You wait over there until your mum arrives.'

She indicated a seat beneath her window which I took until the second her back was turned then I was off, walking very, very quickly out of the main doors until I reached the pavement where I ran flat out towards the Magna.

Chapter Twelve

I made it just as the Magna kids were pouring through the gates. Reggie was easy to spot, despite the hordes piling out of the bus park round him; he was the only one with his head down, looking totally miserable at school ending.

'Cheer up, it might never happen,' I told him, falling into step beside him.

'Brody!' he said, his frown deepening at the sight of me. 'What are you doing here?'

'I wanted to see you. Has your mom really grounded you from the club?'

'Yep,' he said kicking a stone forlornly into the

sidewalk, 'and e-mailing and private phone calls until I apologize for being rude but, seeing as I wasn't rude, I can't apologize for it, so it might take a while.'

'What with stubborn being your middle name and all.'

'It's better than nosy parker,' he replied, referring, I hoped, to his mom, not me.

'What about us?' I asked. 'Where can we meet?'

He glanced round nervously. 'Not here,' he said, 'they don't like Hairy Mary's round here.'

'No worries,' I said. 'Come back to my house. Mom's at the gym, so we'll have privacy and the bus goes straight to your house from outside mine. You'll be home way before your mom gets there.' See, I had it all figured out.

He rubbed his head. 'I dunno . . .'

'Come on, Reggie! Please! I ducked a lesson for you!'

'Did you?'

'Yeah!'

He seemed impressed. 'You'll probably get caned or beheaded or something.'

'At least.'

We began to walk slowly towards the exit to the car park. A girl—I think it was Sammie Wesley's middle sister Sasha—stared curiously at me as she passed. 'I suppose I could come back for a bit,' Reggie began.

'Yes!' I said, overjoyed. It had only been a few days but I had missed him so much.

'. . . but I've got to get home early enough; otherwise I'm dead,' he added.

'No problem. I will not allow tardiness!' I vowed.

'What about you? Aren't you meant to be at After School club?'

'Yeah, but I'll just text Mom to say I'm home already and I'll call Mrs Fryston and make something up.'

'I wish I had a mobile,' Reggie grumbled.

We were home by four fifteen, giving us about an hour together. Reggie wanted us to go in through the back way, in case anyone saw us from the front, seeing as Kirkham Lodge was built so high above the road. Talk about paranoid. It took me ages to unlock the back door—I didn't often use that key and I had to twist the darned thing every which way until it opened, which didn't do much to help Reggie's anxiety. Once inside the kitchen though, Reggie relaxed a little, especially at the mention of food. 'Help yourself to cookies,' I told him.

'Cheers,' he whispered, grinning as he took the whole jar and tucked it under his arm.

'You're welcome,' I whispered back, then asked him why he was still whispering.

'It just seems right,' he whispered again.

'I know what you mean!' I said. 'Let's go to my room. We won't be distracted then if the telephone rings.'

I led the way upstairs, tiptoeing to make a game of it but the truth was I felt as edgy as he did. Even in my own home, it felt a little spooky to be here when I wasn't meant to be. I relaxed a little more once we'd reached my bedroom.

I jumped on to my swivel chair and Reggie sat on my rug, his back against the Edwardian framework of my bed and told me about his mom freaking out when she'd seen us in the hut together. 'But why? Didn't you tell her we were only kissing?' I asked.

'Only? That's enough to bring back hanging in her book.' He wasn't whispering any more but his voice was subdued. His mom must have really torn into him. Weird, huh, how his mom had reacted to us kissing compared to mine. She had phoned Topeka that night. Go figure.

'Your mom was real harsh on the phone,' I said.

'I know, I heard. I was standing about a metre away trying to snatch the thing off her.'

'But what's her problem? She's always been OK with me before.'

'Her problem is she thinks you're about sixteen and I'm about two.'

'Can't you just apologize to her? I don't want

to go to After School club if you're not there,' I told him.

Reggie plunged his hand into the jar for another biscuit. 'Told you! No! Why should I? I'm not saying sorry for something I haven't done. I don't care how long she grounds me for.'

I knew he meant it; Reggie was born stubborn. I swung round in my swivel chair a few more times, trying to think up an idea. 'We could just come back here; not every day, just a couple of times. Or we could meet in town and just hang out in the Ridings Centre,' I suggested.

'I dunno. It's not worth the risk.'

'Hah! So much for not caring what your mum says, tough guy.'

He glowered at me. 'It's all right for you! Your parents are all liberal and laid back. My mum's like a can of pop ready to explode at the tiniest thing these days. And Dad's never around to back me up since he started his new job. He didn't even have time to watch me playing rugby yesterday because he had to catch a flight to some stupid conference. On a Sunday!'

'Tell me about it,' I said, knowing all there was to know about workaholic dads.

'Yeah, well, all I know is if I get caught talking to you I've had it—big time.'

'You'd better go now then,' I said miserably, 'there's not much point in staying here.'

'We could have a last movie-kiss before I go, I suppose,' he suggested, pushing his glasses up the bridge of his nose.

'I suppose one couldn't hurt,' I agreed, leaning down towards him and brushing a biscuit crumb from his top lip. 'Pucker up, sport.'

'If I must,' he said and closed his eyes. That's when I heard the creak.

'What's that?' I hissed.

'What?'

'That noise. I heard something.'

'I didn't hear anything; I was puckering.'

I glanced quickly at the clock. It was four thirty; Mom wouldn't be back yet, surely.

'I heard a creak.'

'Oh, it's probably just a burglar,' Reggie joked. Trouble was, he was right.

Chapter Thirteen

I hadn't fully closed my bedroom door so it was easy to peek through the gap. I couldn't see anything at first; dusk was falling and our landing was gloomy at the best of times. I opened the door wider and listened again. I heard another creak coming up the stairs, then a man's voice whispering something, followed by more creaking. There must be two of them!

I leapt back inside, holding myself rigidly behind my bedroom door, my heart thudding painfully in my chest. Reggie took one look at my face and knew something was wrong. Pointing

to my mobile on the dressing table, I mouthed, 'Dial nine-nine-nine.' He nodded and rose quickly but kicked the glass biscuit jar as he did so, sending it skidding across the floorboards. We may as well have fired a starting pistol.

'What's that?' I heard a stranger ask.

'I don't know.'

'I told you I heard summat earlier.'

'Shh!'

I knew they were just outside my bedroom door. I could feel their shapes like shadows pressing into my skin. Please let them not see us, please let them not see us, I repeated over and over in my head. The door was being pushed slowly open, hiding me. I stopped breathing and squeezed my eyes tight shut. I didn't even know where Reggie was. I hoped he'd hidden.

'Nobody in here,' one of them said with relief.

'Well, I 'eard summat,' the second voice replied

nervously. He didn't sound very old; his voice was still high-pitched and squeaky.

'Best get going anyway—G.K. needs his van back by five.'

'I know, I know! Eh,' the squeakier voice said, 'they're doody. I'll have them.'

I heard footsteps clunk heavily across my bedroom floor but I still had my eyes screwed up so tightly I didn't look to see what he thought were 'doody', whatever that meant.

'Them? They're not worth owt, you nobber, come on. You're going to get us caught!' the other guy hissed. I heard one set of footsteps march off purposefully along the landing and clatter urgently down the stairs, followed by another.

I don't know how long I stood there for; it could have been seconds, it could have been hours. All I know was I had never been so scared in my life. It was Reggie who prised me away from the wall, where I had adhered like a magnet to a fridge.

'They've gone,' he said, his hand shaking as much as mine.

'How do you know?' I whispered.

'They said they had to get the van back by five. It's that now.'

'That doesn't mean anything,' I said, my voice sounding hoarse and distant.

'They've gone, I reckon.'

'You don't know that! We shouldn't move until the police get here. D-did you phone them?'

Reggie shook his head and stammered. 'D-didn't get a chance; after I kicked the jar I dived s-straight under the bed.'

I bit into my lip, totally alarmed that help wasn't on its way.

'Phone . . . phone them now then.'

Reggie nodded, walked over to my dressing table, flicked the lid up on my mobile and then hesitated, before handing it over to me. 'It's probably best if you do it; it's your house,' he said.

I knew I wasn't capable of speaking coherently. 'Can't,' I shook.

'Call your mum then,' he suggested.

I nodded. Mom was on speed dial—I could manage that. I just hoped she wasn't still in the gym with her phone switched off but no, she answered straight away. 'Hi, honey, what's up?' she asked casually.

She freaked when I told her. 'Oh, God!' she said. 'Are you sure they've gone?'

'Think so. *I'm* not certain but . . .'

'God!' she screamed again. 'I'll call the cops. I'll be home in five minutes, Brody. Five minutes! I'm in the juice bar. Don't hang up, I want to keep talking to you . . .' She began barking at the waiter at the juice bar to call the police, garbling out our address and shrieking, 'Tell them there's a kid inside! Tell them my daughter's home alone!' Then she came back to me. 'Brody, Brody, you still there?'

I nodded. 'I can't hear you!' she shrieked.

'I'm here, I'm here,' I reassured her.

'I'm walking out of the fitness centre now and I'm in the car park. I'm walking towards my car. I'm getting into the car . . .'

'Drive safe.'

'I have unlocked the door and am just putting the mobile on hands-free now . . .' she continued.

'You don't have to tell me every little detail,' I hissed at her, though to be honest I did find it comforting listening to her voice.

'She'll be five minutes,' I whispered to Reggie, holding up five fingers.

He held up a scribbled note. I squinted at it like a mole in sunlight, finding it real difficult to listen to hysterical Mom, have a nervous breakdown, and read at the same time.

He held it closer to me. 'Don't say I was here,' the note read.

I shook my head at him furiously. He couldn't do this to me! This was a crisis; even his stuffy mom would understand that. In my ear, my mom told me she was turning left at the traffic lights on Birch Road. 'I'm three minutes away, tops, honey. Three minutes. Move your keister, you loon of a lorry!'

Reggie scribbled another note. 'Please', it read.

'No! What if they're still down there?' I whispered urgently, pointing to the floorboards like a manic woodpecker. He screwed the notes up, stuffed them in his pocket then left—just like that. If Mom hadn't been on the end of the phone, I don't know what I'd have done.

Chapter Fourteen

The police did a great job. They asked Mom to make a list of all the stolen items, warning her she might have to keep adding to it over the next few days as it wasn't always obvious what had been taken at first. Then they searched the whole house, the gardens, the pool, the orchard, the outbuildings. They dusted everywhere for fingerprints, especially my room, even though the only thing missing there were two of my snow globes: my Statue of Liberty and my Empire State Building. Yep, that's what squeaky-voice had taken a fancy to, my snow globes. Why? I mean, if he'd looked thirty centimetres below that, he could have had a brand new, state-of-the-art laptop and cellphone, the dumb speck of low-life scum.

I got real upset when I saw the gap on the windowsill where Liberty had been. I cried a lot. I guess the sobbing helped cover the hesitations I made every two seconds when I was trying to delete Reggie from the scene. 'Yes, I was alone,' I repeated weepily, 'my tooth felt wobbly . . . the veneer seemed to be coming loose and I'm real self-conscious about it so I left school early . . .'

At least I could keep that side of the story consistent.

'But you can't give a description of the men?' WPC Patel asked.

'No; I was too scared to look. All I remember is that one sounded youngish, that's all.'

Mom squeezed my hand real tight.

'Well, every bit helps,' the constable smiled encouragingly but I just felt so pathetic. 'Now,' she said, looking through her notebook again and turning to Mom, 'tell me again about the salesman from this G.K. Vistas company? I want to get the details right.'

Mom began to describe the little bald guy; she'd figured it was him from the outset and told the police so. I knew he wasn't one of the guys in the house but he could have been waiting in the van. It totally figured when you thought about it. Man! He must have thought all his birthdays had come at once when I'd opened the door last week. 'Don't come Mondays because Mom's at the gym then . . .'

Me and my big mouth! I might as well have given him the key and said, 'Help yourself, take whatever you want. Antiques on the left . . . Hi-tech stuff to the right.' That was why I'd had trouble unlocking the door earlier, too. It was already open! Brody the Stupid.

'And one of the men definitely said, "We have to get the van back to G. K. by five"?' the police-woman read out to me.

'Yep.' I nodded.

'I knew it!' Mom fumed. 'I should have followed my instincts and smashed him over the head with that damn bogus picture.'

'Which you don't have any more?' WPC Patel checked.

'No, it went with the garbage.'

'You will get him, won't you?' I asked frantically. 'You will nail him?'

The policewoman looked at me through calm brown eyes. 'We're on to it right now,' she reassured me.

'Good,' I said, 'I hope he gets sent to jail for a million years.'

Dad got home about ten. Mom had called him immediately and he'd dropped everything to catch the first train back. I ran to hug him sooo tightly. I know this sounds kind of sexist and I shouldn't say it but having him home made me feel safer than if it had just been Mom and me. I mean, I love my mom and all and she was a real help on the mobile but Jake's . . . well, my dad. 'It's not what they've taken,' Mom said over my shoulder, 'it's what could have happened to Brody.'

'Don't,' Jake said, his face grey and drawn. 'I've already been on to a security firm in London I've had recommended. They're a top crew; they've worked on a lot of big places. We'll be like Fort Knox by the weekend.'

'That's just what we didn't want,' Mom said sadly, 'that's why we chose to live here in the first place, instead of New York or London.'

'That's life wherever you live, Kierst, the world is full of jerks who'd rather steal other people's property than work for their own. Isn't that right, Brody?'

I nodded. 'Yeah,' I sniffed, 'the world is full of jerks.'

Chapter Fifteen

Get this. Nobody questioned me about missing the last lesson the day before. Mrs Hanson asked how my tooth was in registration and I said, 'Good now, thanks,' and showed her the note Mom had written in my planner. And that was it. Bunking off was a cinch at Queen Mary's. Isn't that ironic? Maybe if I had been caught, none of yesterday would have happened.

During lessons, I was kept so busy I managed to block things out but as soon as school ended I texted Kiersten to check if there was any news from the police. The reply made me almost drop my cellphone. 'Sorry, hon. Not the bald guy.'

I crossed over the road and sank onto the front steps of the art gallery to phone her immediately. 'Mom, what do you mean?' I asked, my voice high and quivery.

'Brody, I'll tell you when you get home.'

'Tell me now!'

I heard her hesitate. 'G. K. Vistas all checked out. Every salesman had an airtight alibi for yesterday, including the bald guy. And G. K. isn't a person—it stands for Grand Kanyon, so they're not thieves, just lousy spellers.'

My head dropped forward like a wilting flower too heavy for its stem. Everything felt too heavy, even the cold March air around me. 'Brody? Brody? Are you still there? Do you want me to fetch you?' Kiersten asked.

'What? No. I'll go to ZAPS. I'll see you at the usual time,' I said and hung up. Home was the last place I wanted to be right now.

The session was in full flow by the time I arrived. I could hear the noise through the thin stud wall partition of the cloakroom. For some reason I tensed up; the noise made me edgy. Sammie, who often looked out for me to arrive, burst through the door and jumped up on to the coat peg bench and grinned at me. 'Hey, Brody.'

I slid off my blazer and yanked my tie loose. 'Hey.'

'Got some good news for ya!'

'Yeah? What's that?'

'Reggie's back.'

'What?' I said, turning to face her.

'Reggie's back; I thought you'd like to know,' she grinned.

I shrugged. 'Oh, that's great,' I said but I wasn't sure how I felt. I know I should have been glad. I mean, the fact that Reggie had turned up meant he'd swallowed his pride and apologized to his mom for me. But . . . oh, I couldn't think straight. If the robbers had been arrested, I know I would have gone up to Reggie and shared the news. We could have swapped stories about what had happened. Turned it into an adventure. But not now.

The main picture that kept flashing in my head

as I sorted through my bag was of Reggie, my best buddy, my boyfriend for over a year, the person I had felt closest to in the whole world, shoving a stupid note in my face. 'Don't tell anyone.' Pathetic! No way would I have done that if it had been the other way round, no matter what the consequences. No way.

He'd let me down big style.

I took a long, long time to sort out my things. I didn't even realize I was pummelling my untouched lunch bag of potato chips into smithereens until Sammie pointed it out. 'I'll have 'em if you don't want 'em,' she offered.

I handed her the pulped bag. 'Are you in a mardy about something?' she asked.

'Yeah,' I said, 'you could say that.'

Chapter Sixteen

Reggie was over in Boff Corner, chatting and laughing with Lloyd and Sam as he always did. The guy without a care in the world. He looked across as soon as I entered and waved. I marched over to him but didn't sit down. 'So, you're alive then?' I asked him pointedly.

The others, thinking I was referring to his absence from here the past few days, smirked.

'Good to see you, too!' he retorted, trying to make a joke of my coldness. I could tell from his eyes he was hurt but what did he expect? He could have been floating with the fish in the Calder since last night for all I knew.

I did a sharp U-turn and went and parked myself as far away from him as I could which happened to be with Mrs McCormack and her craft table dudes.

'Well hello, Brody,' Mrs McCormack said in surprise as I pulled out a chair, 'nice to see you here.'

'Thanks,' I muttered. I was not a regular—Mrs McCormack's ideas are usually a bit lame, to be honest.

'Help yourself to a cereal box. We're designing giant book covers for our display to go with the Big Book Quiz.' She smiled. See what I mean?

'Mine's called *Captain No Underpants*,' Brandon declared, scribbling something round and purposeful on his sheet with a thick wax crayon.

'Erm . . . that's neat,' I said.

'You can copy if you like. I don't mind,' he told me generously.

I softened then. Brandon was only six and had been through some tough times; I could hardly be grouchy with him. 'Thanks, cool guy,' I said and reached across for a Frosties carton. Well, why not? Scribbling rubbish on a sheet of sugar paper and sticking it on to a cereal box was just the kind of activity a girl needed when she'd dumped her boyfriend.

Chapter Seventeen

The next few days were horrible. I couldn't accept that maybe it would take a while to find the guys who broke into the house; even worse to think the police might *never* catch them. In my head, that meant the pair were free to come waltzing into Kirkham Lodge any old time they chose and nothing either Kiersten, Jake, or WPC Patel could say to me made me change my mind.

I wasn't getting much sleep so my energy levels were really low; I was in a fog half the time. School was bearable because nobody knew about what had happened so I could go about my business more or less as normal. If anything, I worked harder, just to keep my brain busy, and my friends teased me about not peaking too soon for the Endeavour Trophy given out at the end of Upper Fourth. The harder I worked at school, the more drained I felt at the end of the day, though, so After School club was a little more difficult to get through, especially with the Reggie thing.

He had tried to talk to me a couple of times but I just blanked him whenever he came near. Then he'd resorted to asking kids like Lloyd and Sammie to act as go-betweens but I wasn't interested. He even used Ruby a couple of times, sending her with little folded notes which she tried to hand over with great ceremony but which I threw straight in the trash. 'That's rude!' she said crossly the last time it happened.

'Bite me, Ruby,' I snapped at her.

But it was being home that I found most stressful of all. As soon as the car pulled up the drive, I'd remember every single thing from that Monday afternoon, from struggling to open the back door with Reggie to Mom coming home and pulling me close. I could manage the kitchen, just about, and the downstairs generally but when it came to bedtime I just went into meltdown. No way would I even enter my bedroom. Instead I spent the night with Kiersten and Jake in their room, feeling like a little baby, but I just couldn't help it.

At first, Dad kept it light, saying he was too old for camping on floors and begging me to take pity on his 'bad back'. When that didn't work he changed tactics, saying I couldn't let low-life 'win' like this but I absolutely refused to return. I never wanted to sleep or even go in that creepy room again. In the end, we compromised and I had all my stuff moved into the guest bedroom but only after I had spoken on the phone to WPC Patel personally and she had assured me the intruders hadn't gone in there at all.

Mom and Orla sorted everything out for me while I was at school, transferring all my clothes and bedding and books from my old room to my new one. I instructed Mom to leave behind all my snow globes though; I didn't want those any more. Who knew how many of them Squeaky Voice had touched before taking Liberty? Orla had wrapped them in newspaper and taken them to a charity shop. 'She  was so upset,' Mom told me, 'saying what a shame a young girl had to throw away her favourite things because of two cabbage heads.'

Yep, lady, it sure was.

On Saturday, when Dad suggested he might go back to London the following Monday, I totally lost control, crying and pleading until he promised he wouldn't go until at least all the security system had been fitted. After exchanging meaningful looks with Kiersten, something that happened a lot these days, he agreed.

I hated feeling like this; I was surprised at myself for reacting like some wuss. I mean, the burglars hadn't taken that much, or done any damage, or hurt me physically but no matter how many times I reminded myself of that, I still felt scared and insecure. I knew I'd be like this until the burglars had been caught; only then could I be Brody Miller again.

Chapter Eighteen

The following Monday at After School club, I was trying to make a bookmark at the craft table when Mrs Fryston asked for the Big Book Quiz team to go over to the book corner. I didn't hear at first; I was half-asleep and it wasn't until Alex tapped me on the shoulder and told me they were waiting I even moved. Yawning, I set my sequins and beads aside and mooched across to the others. I slumped down on the purple couch next to Alex, facing Lloyd and Sam on bean bags opposite and tried to look attentive when Mrs Fryston began to speak. 'Right then. The next round is on Thursday and we'll be going to Anston After School club for that. Let's just hope it's better organized this time, eh? You'll need to get these consent forms signed so you can travel in my car with me . . .'

She began dishing out sheets of paper. As I took mine, my stomach clenched. It hadn't occurred to me we'd be travelling somewhere else to participate and the idea made me anxious. Everything was even more upside down at home now; the security guys had arrived last night and were already banging away when I left this morning. I didn't want to do anything different here; I wanted to stay put.

'Round Two is "Pick a Peck of Poets",' Mrs F. continued. 'You've all had the four poems, haven't you? I just need to know who's doing what.'

'I haven't,' I said.

'You have,' Sam replied. 'You said you'd do any so we gave you "Matilda".'

It was news to me. '"Matilda"?'

Sam nodded. 'Matilda told such dreadful lies. It made one Gasp and Stretch one's Eyes. Hilaire Belloc. It's a good one.'

'I don't remember,' I said.

85

'I left it next to you the other day,' Alex said, 'I knew you hadn't heard me.'

'Why didn't you say something then, stupid?' I snapped. 'How am I supposed to enter a competition if I don't have the material?'

Alex looked at me and bit her lip. 'I'm sorry, Brody, I thought you'd seen it . . . I bet Mum's put it somewhere, I'll just go ask.'

'Don't bother,' I said, making my mind up instantly, 'I'm not going. I quit.'

'Brody . . .' Mrs Fryston began but I jumped up before she could come out with any of the bull she was planning on coming out with.

'Don't!' I yelled at her. 'Don't even try! I'm sick of doing you favours! Find some other loser and leave me alone!'

I strode back to the craft table and helped myself to a handful of beads, leaving them with their dumbstruck faces and stupid poems.

Mrs Fryston didn't say anything to me for the rest of the session or anything to Mom when she picked me up but she did call home later that evening. She had a long, long talk to my mom and I heard Mom telling her about the burglary and how I'd been 'affected' by it and how she was 'concerned' about me. That irritated me beyond belief. Hello, mother! Don't *I* get any say in who knows my business any more? When Mom came off the phone I totally flipped out again. 'Thanks, Kiersten! Thanks a bunch! Tell the whole world about me, why don't you! Maybe you should take out a page in the paper and let the nation know how your daughter can't sleep in her own bed any more!' I yelled at her.

She looked at me with her big, sad eyes. 'Brody,' she said, 'where have you gone?'

Chapter Nineteen

Not surprisingly people kept their distance in the mobile after that. They backed off, leaving me to my sequins and bad-ass attitude. Part of me felt mortified. I had been so rude and mean, especially to Mom and Alex and Mrs Fryston but—and it was hard for me to admit to this—part of me found it kind of liberating. No more 'Brody, can you help me with this?' 'Brody, would you mind taking over that?' Like when the outlaw came into town in cowboy films, little kids were dragged out of the way as I walked across the floor. There were hasty whispers, secret glances wherever I went. Even queues melted away when I joined them—I would find myself suddenly standing at the front of the line, my candy pre-packaged and ready to go. Such power!

I did feel bad on Thursday, though, when Mrs Fryston called for the Big Book Quiz team to get ready. Check this out—nobody had volunteered to take my place so only three of them were going. Instead, Sam had volunteered to recite both his poem and mine. 'It'll be a cinch,' I overheard him saying to Alex, 'I was born for this.' I hoped so.

I wanted to say good luck with everyone else when they waved the team off, especially when I saw Lloyd's nervous-looking face peer out of the side of the minibus, but I daren't. I thought they'd think I was being a hypocrite or sarcastic or something. Then I defended myself by thinking, why should I be supportive? Nobody was supportive for me, were they, *Reggie*?

Inside the mobile, the noise level had immediately increased on Mrs Fryston's departure. It wasn't even a particularly busy afternoon; there were only about ten kids in attendance with Mrs McCormack and Mr Wesley supervising but without the Super's calming but firm influence everyone became a little more boisterous. I could feel my nerves jangling already.

I don't need to tell you who was the most boisterous. Ruby was in one of her 'hyper' states, darting from one end of the room to the other, throwing cushions, knocking things over. Mrs McCormack tried to involve her in helping to pour squash into beakers but that was too lame for Ruby. 'Don't want to,' she said and flounced over to Mucky Mick's cage, which wasn't far from where I was sitting, reading a magazine, trying to mind my own business. I had swapped the craft table for magazines and books recently because they were easier to hide behind

and cut the risk of any eye-to-eye with Reggie. I had no mixed feelings where *he* was concerned.

Ruby seemed to quieten down for a minute, happy to engage the hamster in a conversation about his likes and dislikes. 'What did you say your favourite colour was again?' I heard her ask. 'Mine's black.'

Now there's a surprise, I thought. This was quickly followed by another surprise as Ruby let out a delighted squeal and shouted, 'Look! Look! Mucky Mick's going on holiday!' I felt something run across my feet and then it was all systems go as everyone fell on to all fours and began the hunt for the fleeing hamster.

'Close all the doors!' Mrs McCormack ordered.

It turns out hamsters are awesome at hide-and-seek. After twenty minutes we still hadn't found the thing. I was getting bored and knee-ache and decided once I'd inched my way along the purple couch for the fifth time I'd call it a day. I was halfway along when I cracked heads with someone coming in the opposite direction. I looked up to find Reggie there, an inch from my face, grinning—yes—grinning at me.

'Oh, it's you,' I snarled.

'Well spotted.'

Still on all fours, I moved to the right. He did

the same, blocking my path. 'Don't go,' he said, 'I wanted to ask you something.'

'What?'

'Have they found him yet?'

'Would I still be down here ruining my tights if they had?' I asked sharply.

'Not the hamster,' Reggie said, patting his trouser pocket, 'I know where he is! I meant the toe-rag burglar with the divvy baseball boots.'

'Baseball boots? What baseball boots?'

Reggie glanced round and leaned so close the tip of his nose almost touched mine. 'The one who came into the bedroom had these naff base-ball boots on with those crappy green and black zigzag patterns up the sides all the Townies are wearing.'

'What else? What else was he wearing?' I asked, grabbing Reggie's wrist.

He shook his head. 'Nothing else. I don't mean

he was starkers, I mean that's all I saw that time. I was under the bed, remember.'

I let go of him as if I'd been stung. 'Yeah, I remember. I'm amazed you do though,' I sneered, 'I mean, you weren't even there, were you? You were "miles away"!'

'Fair-do's, Brody. I messed up, but if you just let me apolo—'

But I was already on my feet. 'Save it for someone who gives a hoot, Reggie,' I hissed and walked away.

Chapter Twenty

Just because I wasn't speaking to Reggie it didn't mean I couldn't use his information, though. As soon as I got in the car, I told Mom about the boots.

She frowned. 'How can you remember that, hon? I thought you were behind the door the whole time?'

'Shoot! I just did, that's all,' I said irritably. 'We can phone the police as soon as we get home and let them know.'

Mom pulled away from the kerb. 'Mm. I doubt they'd see it as much of a breakthrough; that zigzag pattern is pretty popular . . .'

Trust her to know about fashion trends! Like it mattered. 'It's a clue! Of course it's a break-through!' I yelled.

Mom put her foot on the brake and stopped the car immediately, pulling me round by the shoulders to make me look at her. 'Hey! All I was meaning was don't get your hopes up; it's not a lot to go on. And please don't talk to me like that. I know you're upset but I'm not the bad guy here.'

'Fine,' I said, twisting away, 'I won't speak to you at all.'

I kept up the silent treatment all the way home. While Mom put the car away, I headed straight into the house, hoping Dad would be a bit more open-minded about my information. For once I didn't have to go roaming through the whole house to find him; he was already in the kitchen when I flounced in. Trouble was, Orla was there too, polishing away at one of Mom's cherished vases and chatting ten-to-the-dozen.

I groaned inwardly. I'd forgotten the cleaner

would be there. She had agreed to change her hours temporarily to work in the evenings; there was too much dust and commotion with the security guys around during the day. I said hello to her and kissed Dad on the cheek then launched straight in. 'Jake,' I said, 'I've just remembered something about one of the burglars I think the police should know straightaway . . .'

'That's grand,' Orla interrupted, 'the sooner those crooks are found the better, coming in and terrorizing little girls in broad daylight. They should have the backside tanned off them, if you want my opinion . . .'

I gave Orla an appreciative smile. She'd been on my side since day one. 'Anyway,' I continued hurriedly, in case Mom blew in, 'one of them was wearing baseball boots with green and black zigzags up the sides.'

Before Dad could respond there was an ear-shattering crashing sound as Orla dropped the vase onto the tiled floor and it smashed to smithereens.

Chaos! Dad started barking orders about not

treading on the
sharp edges and
Orla apologized
about a million
times and went to
find a dustpan and
brush. Of course,

Kiersten came in and added to the chaos by
standing right on a chunk of the thing and
pounding it into dust. By the time the floor had
been cleared and Orla had gone home and Dad
had moaned about 'something else to claim on
the insurance', Reggie's information about zigzag
baseball boots had been relegated to the minor
leagues. I did manage to get a promise out of my
folks that they'd let WPC Patel know about it
though, first thing in the morning.

I thought I would sleep better but now that I
had an image of the boots, I built up a picture of
the guy wearing them, ankles upward. He was
real tall—at least six-two—and had a mean, craggy
face framed by lank, oily hair. His teeth were
yellow from smoking too much dope and his

breath was foul and rancid. I dreamt of him leaning over my bed, the snow globe in his hand, laughing in my face. 'I'm coming to get you, Brody Miller. All the fancy technology in the world won't keep me out, and that's a promise.'

Chapter Twenty-One

Friday was a weird day at school. It started during English when Miss Hogenboom wanted to confiscate my cellphone. OK, I admit I was texting home when I should have been annotating some passage or other but Miss Hogenboom could have given me a warning instead of just demanding I hand it over. 'I am sick and tired of these things. Why they are even allowed on the premises I'll never know,' she said, holding out her hand oh-so-sure I was going to just give up my phone to her without an argument. No way, ma'am. Not today. Not possible. 'I promise I won't text anyone again but I need to keep it,' I pleaded, thrusting it quickly into my bag.

'I don't bargain, dear,' she said.

Again I refused, despite everyone staring at me in dismay—being smart with Miss Hogenboom was not recommended—but I couldn't let my phone go. What if Mom called? After about ten minutes of raising her blood pressure way above the recommended limits for a lady her age but getting nowhere with me, Miss Hogenboom sent me to Mrs Hanson. Same scenario. Mrs Hanson sent me to Mrs Williams-Pryce, the head of year. Same scenario. I was as amazed as my teachers at what Mrs Hanson called my 'obduracy' but no way was I handing over my cellphone. No way. Incidentally, obduracy is no way as cool a word as tardy, is it?

After a stern lecture on manners and the importance of rules, which reduced me to tears but still wouldn't make me yield my cellphone, an exasperated Mrs Williams-Pryce called home and spoke to Jake. I guessed from the amount of incoming head nodding and sympathetic clucking he must have told her the whole sorry story of the burglary

and how his daughter had gone flaky as a result. Cool. Now everyone at school knew as well as everyone at After School club but I was way past caring. 'Did he say anything about baseball boots?' I asked her when she finally got off the phone.

No, was the short, puzzled answer. After a bit of nose-blowing on my part and a story of how her brother had been burgled and it's not a very nice experience is it, on her part, Mrs Williams-Pryce allowed me to keep my cellphone, providing I didn't use it ever again during lessons for the rest of my school life. I then had to apologize to Mrs Hanson and Miss Hogenboom, which was fine by me, and catch up on all the classwork I'd missed which was less fine but totally fair.

Friday got even weirder when school ended. Reggie was waiting for me. 'What do you want?'

I said, irritated that even now I couldn't check my texts in peace.

'Oh, I was just passing,' he said, falling into step beside me.

'Keep passing then,' I advised as I checked out messages in my inbox—nada—and punched an angry message to Kiersten.

'Oh, come on, you've got to talk to me sometime, you miserable mare.'

'Drop dead, Reggie.'

'OK,' he said and flung himself onto the sidewalk.

And I mean flung. Straight down, with no safety net to stop him smashing his face to pieces on the flagstones. Girls scattered as he plunged, muttering the word 'idiot'; a car slowed down to check what was going on, the woman driver with a concerned look on her face. 'Reggie, get up,' I said, standing by his spread-eagled limbs, waving the driver on with a phoney smile before continuing my text. 'Get up!' I repeated when there was no movement.

'Can't. I'm dead,' he replied.

'Fine. The hospital's over the road; I'm sure they'll have a spare place in the morgue for you,' I informed him and walked off.

I'd got about fifty metres when he found me again. 'Oh, we are playing tough, aren't we?' he muttered.

'I'm not playing anything.'

'Well, at least you're talking, that's something, I suppose.'

I glanced sideways at him. He had shards of grit stuck to his neck and there was a leaf sticking out of his shirt collar. Looking good, Reggie. 'Why are you here? Won't your mummy be angry with you?' I asked as we waited for the traffic to stop on Bond Street so we could cross.

'I want to talk.'

'We've got nothing to talk about.'

'Course we have—you're not the only one who's scared, you know.'

'Meaning?'

'Meaning just that!'

I was kind of surprised at Reggie's admission; he's usually *so* in touch with his masculine side.

'I keep wondering if they saw me,' he added more quietly.

'From under the bed?'

Magna Boy didn't seem put off by my sarcasm. 'Well, you never know. He might have had X-ray vision or miniature cameras in his boots or something,' he mumbled.

It sounded stupid and we both knew it but, annoyingly, I totally understood. It doesn't help to have a vivid imagination sometimes. I looked closely at Reggie and knew from the glum expression on his face he was being sincere. 'What do you think he looked like? The one who came into my room?' I asked more quietly. 'I think he was a dope-head with long, greasy hair and yellow teeth,' I said.

Reggie fell into step beside me. 'Nah—he'd be that skinhead kind—you know—a number one haircut and into all the designer gear. Maybe that's what they were after—clothes and things.'

'I still don't get why he took my snow globes.'

'Like the other bloke said, he was a "nobber".'

I gave a short laugh and we continued to exchange ideas all the way to the bus station. It was such a relief to share the nightmare with him. He'd been there; he understood. Our bus was waiting and Reggie automatically stood to one side to allow me on first. Without thinking I made my way to the long side seat—our usual—and Reggie sat next to me. It was amazing how all my animosity towards him was draining away.

He dumped his bag on the space between us and looked straight at me. 'I'm really sorry for leaving you that day, Brody. I wasn't thinking straight. I just had it in my head I had to get home before Mum found out where I'd been.'

'I know,' I said, seeing clearly for the first time what a lousy position he'd been in. Why should he have stayed just to get into a deeper mess, really? After all, I'd been the one who brought him home in the first place. I had put him in danger, not the other way round.

'What would your mom say if she saw you here now?' I asked, remembering the things she had said to me on the phone.

'I don't know and I don't care,' Reggie said. 'All I know is it's where I want to be.'

I looked at Reggie and he looked at me and it felt like such a long, long time since we'd exchanged movie-kisses in the equipment shed. I reached out my hand and pulled the leaf out of his collar.

Chapter Twenty-Two

We entered the After School club together. 'Cover up, dude,' I warned Reggie as Ruby charged straight for us.

'Already on it,' he replied, shielding himself with his school bag.

Ruby let out a mighty howl as her head clashed against canvas and textbooks. 'That hurt!' she cried, rubbing her head angrily and stamping her feet in true drama queen style.

'Go play, Rubes,' Reggie told her, sounding really fed up.

'Brandon's free by the dressing-up gear,' I added.

'Brandon smells of wee,' she retorted.

'Looks like he's going straight for the cowboy boots, too,' I lied.

Ruby scowled at me. 'He can't wear them; they're mine,' she said and stalked over to stake her claim, not realizing until she got there Brandon was nowhere near. She sat on the floor and began to put the boots on anyway, absorbed in getting her feet into them before anyone else did.

'Great teamwork,' I laughed, giving Reggie a high-five. He returned it, looking straight into my eyes. 'I'm going to talk to Mum. I'll tell her everything.'

'You don't have to,' I said.

'Yeah, I do. It's like having a massive Sunday dinner in my stomach that won't digest. I feel full and bloated all the time.'

'Nice comparison,' I smiled.

'I thought so,' he replied smugly, 'though I can't

tell her tonight—she's got to pick Dad up from the airport. I'll tell her tomorrow. Promise.'

'It's up to you.'

We both stood there, a little unsure as to what to do next. I had my magazine ready and there were plenty of vacant places over by the craft table but I really wanted to be with Reggie; I wanted us to be friends again. I daren't *say* that, though. Luckily it was Reggie who broke the ice, asking me if I was coming to sit in Boff Corner. 'You can do my French for me,' he said generously.

'Oh, gee, *merci beaucoup*,' I replied.

'It's murky buckets, actually,' Reggie corrected, leading the way. 'If you don't even know the basics, I might as well do it myself.'

'Well, that'll make a change.'

'Says you. Bet you're bottom of maths these days.'

'Near to the top, actually.'

'Yeah, and pigs might fly.'

'I hope one poops on your head as it passes over.'

Oh, it was so good to be bantering again!

As we approached the table, razor-eyed Sammie nudged Sam who nudged Lloyd who looked up from his drawing, smiled, then looked back down again.

'Budge over,' Reggie told Lloyd, who duly inched his way along the bench.

I felt a little strange being there again, almost as if I were intruding. And I had been real mean to them. What if they didn't want me back? 'Oh! How did it go last night?' I asked, noticing Lloyd had his printed poetry sheet close by. Neat, neutral opening topic, I figured.

'Rubbish,' he began, 'for a start . . .'

An elbow from Sam sent Lloyd's pencil skidding over his sheet. 'We got through to the final; that's the main thing, right? Brody doesn't need to know the details,' Sam said pointedly to him.

'Right,' Lloyd mumbled, frowning ferociously back at Sam.

In other words, butt out, Brody, this is none of your business now. Wow! My standing at Boff Corner really had nose-dived, but what could I expect? I just congratulated them on getting through and began unloading my homework onto the table. Reggie helpfully added to the pile by sliding me his French book. 'Page fifteen, numbers one to eleven. Sea view play.'

'Murky buckets,' I replied.

It was good to be back, kind of.

Chapter Twenty-Three

Weird Friday wasn't over yet, though. Dad picked me up that evening, which was great but unexpected. 'Where's Mom?' I asked immediately.

'Well, nice to see you, too,' he said, taking my bag and nodding goodbye to Mrs Fryston.

'She's OK, isn't she? Only she hasn't texted me today and . . .'

'She's fine, she's fine,' Jake reassured me, ferrying me out, 'she's just having domestics with the domestic.'

'What do you mean?'

'Mrs Voyle's decided to hand her notice in. Well,

not even that, actually. She wants to leave after her stint tonight. Half the house covered in plaster and dust from the workmen and she decides to drop us in it. Charming. People have no sense of loyalty these days. It's the same in London. These people arrive from agencies with a list of rules longer than the Magna Carta. They can't do this and they mustn't lift that . . .'

I followed Dad all the way to the car only half listening to his ranting. It wasn't fair, though. Just as one thing got smoothed out, something else came along to spoil it. I liked Orla, too; she was always cheerful and kind and funny. Life sucked.

When we arrived back, I just said a quick 'Hi' to Mom. Jake had advised me to keep a low profile until we knew how negotiations had gone. From the grunt of a response Mom gave me, and the way she was whacking tonight's steak with the mallet, not too good was the answer. I kept right on walking.

Orla was wiping the walnut casing of the longcase clock in the hallway, where the final bits of plaster from the ceiling had left a fine film of dust everywhere. 'Hi, Orla,' I said cautiously.

She didn't even glance up at me. Instead, she started going at the plinth of the clock with her duster as if it hadn't been polished for two centuries. An awful thought crossed my mind. Was Orla going because of me? Because I'd been so sassy lately?

'Erm . . . I'm real sorry to hear about you leaving us . . .' I began.

'Yes, well, these things happen,' she mumbled.

'And I'm sorry for being rude lately. It's not personal, it's just that since the . . . you know . . .' I stared up at the new sensors in the ceiling, protruding diligently from all corners.

'I know!' Orla wailed then let out this strangled cry that sent goosebumps up and down my arms. It was awful.

'Orla? Orla, what's wrong?' I asked, dropping my schoolbag and rushing across to her.

She couldn't answer. I sat her down on a chair and dashed into the kitchen to fetch a glass of water. 'Orla's crying!' I yelled to Jake and Kiersten. 'Bring Kleenex!'

'It's all my fault, it's all my fault,' Orla sobbed, as we gathered round.

'What is?' Kiersten asked, kneeling in front of the cleaner and rubbing the back of her hand gently.

'I kept it. Oh, I wish to God and all the Saints in Heaven with Him I hadn't. I wish I'd thrown it in the rubbish like you told me but they wouldn't take it away you see. Said if it didn't fit in the bin, they weren't interested . . .'

'Who? What?'

'Those bin men. They wouldn't take the picture. The lovely aerial photo of the house.'

'So?' Kiersten asked.

Orla blew hard into the tissue I had offered her. 'So I took it home with me and I put it above my mantelpiece. "There you go", I said to our Robert, "that'll be us one day when we win the Lotto."' She laughed bitterly.

'Well,' Mom began, 'I wish you hadn't done that, Orla, but OK, it's no big deal.'

'Oh, it is, Mrs Miller,' Orla sobbed, 'it's enormous!'

Chapter Twenty-Four

Turned out she was right; it was enormous. After a couple of minutes and a hundred sips of water, the distraught lady pulled herself together and told us the real reason she'd handed in her notice. Remember how she'd dropped the ceramic vase when I mentioned the zigzag patterns on the baseball boots? Want to know why? Robert had some boots exactly the same. Want to know what else—and I'm telling you this a whole lot quicker than Orla told us, believe me—it was Robert and this other guy who'd broken into the house. No kidding!

Apparently Robert, between jobs and as

'fickless' as ever, often had mates round to the house when she was out. One day she'd got home from work and Robert and his friend Marley had taken the photograph of Kirkham Lodge down and were examining it with a magnifying glass. 'Just checking out the ridges and guttering, seeing if there's a job in it,' Marley had explained. He often got 'backhanders' from some guy called Gary Kaye, a roofer, if he found jobs for him. Yep, you've got it—G. K.—a builder, but more importantly a van owner. Oh, it all fitted so neatly when you thought about it. Not that Orla had thought much more about it until after the robbery.

Then she started to notice a change in Robert's behaviour. Every time she talked about what had happened at our house—and to me in particular—he'd either change the subject or look sheepish and sullen, especially when she mentioned me moving out of my bedroom and being 'scared of my own shadow'. So she already had an inkling something was wrong but it was hearing about the boots that was the clincher.

Orla had gone home and searched her son's room and found—you've guessed it—my snow globes hidden in the bottom of his wardrobe. As soon as he'd come home from the pub, she'd confronted him. He'd denied it at first but she'd kept on and on until she'd worn him down and he admitted he'd borrowed her side-door key to let himself in. 'So what are you going to do? Shop me? Your own son?' he'd asked her. 'In tears he was; tears as big as balloons.' Orla had looked up at us then, shaking her head in disbelief. 'He's right! I can't hand my own son over to the police, though Lord knows he deserves it but he's all I've got in the world since Jimmy died. What shall I do? What shall I do?' It seemed an odd thing to be asking us.

Mind you, our answer was even more odd.

Chapter Twenty-Five

'You did what?' Reggie asked in astonishment when I phoned him a couple of hours later and told him the whole saga.

'Invited them to have tea,' I repeated. 'I know it sounds crazy but see, Orla was so upset we agreed we wouldn't bring the police in just yet; not until we'd heard what Robert had to say for himself. If he doesn't show, we go straight to the cops. End of.'

'Let me get this straight. This woman, this Orla Voyle—which is a totally made-up name by the way . . .'

'No it isn't.'

'Think about it. *Orla Voyle.* What's her husband called? Popeye?'

'Her husband's dead and he was called Jimmy. They were childhood sweethearts; he died when Robert was ten and Robert hasn't been the same since.'

'Whatever. This woman sits there and admits her son and his mate burgled your house, nicked your stuff, frightened you—and me—to death and you're inviting them back to the house for a cup of tea and a biscuit?'

'Not the house,' I said hastily, 'I don't want them in the house again. We're meeting in the Cyber Rooms café off the Bull Ring at four o'clock tomorrow. That's one reason I'm phoning—I didn't want you turning up outside Queen Mary's and wondering what was going on . . . that's if you were planning on turning up?'

'Course I was,' he said firmly which made me feel all fluttery inside. 'Why do you have to go, though? Why can't they all sort it out between them? What if he's armed or something?'

'I . . . I hadn't thought of that. I don't think he will be . . . Orla swears he's never done anything like this before.'

'She would.'

'Reggie, don't be so negative.'

'Well, someone's got to give you a reality check. Talk about backtracking; one minute you're having nightmares about this geezer, the next you're his best mate.'

'I know it sounds weird,' I admitted, 'but it's just now that I know who did it, I don't feel as . . . as spooked. I've got a name, an age, a reason— kind of. Do you know he took the snow globes to give to his niece because he couldn't afford anything for her birthday?'

'What kind of an excuse is that? Who wants nicked stuff for a birthday present?'

I hadn't looked at it like that. It had all seemed so simple when Orla was here, begging us to give her son a chance because he'd never had a break. But what Reggie was saying was right, too. I felt the new confidence I'd built up begin to crumble. I tried again, to convince myself as much as

Reggie. 'Well, Mom read this information on the net, about these case studies, where victims come face to face with the criminals and apparently it can help the healing process.'

'Are you allowed to smack them one?' Reggie asked. 'That'd help tons.'

'I'm pretty sure that's not part of the deal.'

'Pity.'

I had intended to ask him if he wanted to come too. I'd confessed to Mom about him being with me that day, explaining why I had kept it quiet, and she said I should invite him. 'Providing he gets permission,' she had stipulated. But I got the feeling having Reggie there in this mood might not help the healing process. 'I'd better go,' I said, 'don't want your mom coming home and catching you talking to that Brody Miller girl.'

He didn't disagree. 'Yeah, well, anyway, tell me what happens tomorrow, won't you?'

'You'll be the first to know,' I promised.

Chapter Twenty-Six

We turned up at the Cyber Rooms for the meeting as planned. Orla had already telephoned ahead to let us know Marley wouldn't be there—he had 'commitments'—so we knew it would just be the two of them and the three of us. I saw Orla immediately at the far end of the café. She was all dressed up in what I guessed was her best navy blue suit and, to top it off, a matching hat. The outfit was a little out of place, especially among the mainly studenty types around her, and it touched me deeply that she'd felt it necessary to wear it. I did like Orla so much. Shame her son had to spoil everything.

He was sitting next to her. Robbing Robert, in the flesh. He was also dressed in a suit; under orders, no doubt. They looked like two lost wedding guests. I didn't feel sorry for him, though. All day, Reggie's warnings had been flashing through my head. What if he *was* armed? What if it *was* all a set up? I ducked behind Mom, wishing I'd never listened to her theories about victims and stupid face-to-face encounters. It wasn't even *me* she was concerned about. 'Jake,' Mom hissed as we approached the table, 'remember what I said: keep calm. If you lose it like you did at Christmas, *we'll* end up in trouble and then you've blown it as far as the courts go.'

'As if I needed telling,' Dad snapped. I got the idea they were both as tense as I was—it didn't help.

Now we were nearer, I could make out Robert's features more clearly. Like Orla he had a long face with even but unimposing features; he would not stand out in a crowd. His light brown hair was short but not closely cropped like Reggie had imagined. He wasn't like I had imagined, either.

I didn't know whether to feel glad or disappointed. For the record, I didn't know what to feel at all. It was all a bit surreal.

Orla nudged Robert so that he sprang rather than rose out of his seat, banging into the people on the table behind him. 'Sorry, mate,' he muttered to them.

Hearing that squeaky voice again turned my stomach. In an instant I was behind my old bedroom door again, terrified. I would have run away if Mom hadn't been holding my hand fast. She steered me to the table where I sat in rigid silence next to Orla.

It was Dad who did all the talking initially. At first, Robert just grunted or mumbled defensive responses to Jake's probing questions and I just sat there like a timid little rabbit. Orla was quiet, too, squeezing her handbag like a heart surgeon testing for signs of life. I focused gratefully on my cappuccino when it arrived, watching the pale bubbly froth until it disappeared.

'Brody?' Kiersten asked me.

I glanced up at her, realizing from her worried expression it couldn't have been the first time she'd called my name. I must have tuned out; I do that sometimes when I'm anxious. 'Brody, do you have anything you want to ask? Anything you want to tell this . . . guy?' she said, her eyebrows raised, encouraging me to unload. I shook my head. I had seen him. I could put a face to the monster; that was enough. I had nothing I wanted to tell this . . . guy, after all.

'Robert!' Orla suddenly snapped. 'What have *you* got to say to Brody?'

I felt his eyes on me. I didn't want to look at him, not really, but I forced myself to, because otherwise there would have been no point in coming, in going through this whole charade. I slowly raised my head and stared into his eyes and saw enough shame in them to persuade me to keep on looking. He cleared his throat nervously. 'Well,' he began, 'well, like . . .' I held his gaze steadily, like a nurse determined her patient would take his medicine, even though it took me every shred of every nerve I had in my entire body to do it. Maybe Robert was feeling and thinking the same: get it over and done with, because he began to speak rapidly, straight at me, in broad Yorkshire. I caught the gist of it, just about. 'I . . . I'm sorry, like, for scaring you. I didn't think nobody'd be in, like, do you know what I'm saying? I wouldn't have done owt . . . hurt you or owt. Marley wouldn't either—we're not like that—he's got a kid of 'is own, and another on the way, do you know what I mean?'

He glanced away and began to fidget with the bowl of white and brown sugar cubes in front of him before taking a deep breath and continuing. 'If we'd have known you was upstairs we wouldn't have gone up. I swear. It freaked me out when Mam told us you was there all the time. I'm telling you, if I'd have seen you I'd have died on the spot. No kidding—I mean, look at me—I'm a right wimp. The idea was just to have a sneck round in private, like, to see what the inside of a big house looked like.'

'Oh, please!' Mom snapped.

Robert's face reddened instantly when he realized no one believed that crock for a second. 'We never meant no 'arm,' he finished lamely.

Now that part I did believe. Reggie would probably call me a sucker, but I did believe he wouldn't have broken in if he'd known I was inside at the time. He'd still have broken in, but another time. Robert Voyle was, in his own words, a right wimp.

All the fear that I had stored up in my insides since the break-in dissolved slowly and completely like sugar crystals in boiling water.

I nodded to him once, briefly, just long enough for him to know I'd got the message. He nodded back.

'I want to go now,' I announced abruptly to Kiersten, 'I'm done.'

I stood up, ready to leave. Everyone looked a bit confused, like when you come out of a dark cinema into sunshine, but I didn't want to be part of the next stage. The deciding whether to go to the police or not part—that was strictly for the grown-ups. I just wanted to go to After School club and be normal.

'Wait,' Robert said, 'I want to give you these back.' He scrambled beneath the table for a carrier bag which he held out like a fisherman exhibiting a prize catch. 'It's them things . . .' he explained.

'I know what they are,' I said. 'No offence but they'd creep me out if I touched them now. You keep them. Give them to . . .' I was going to say 'your niece' but remembered Reggie's thoughts on that. '. . . Marley's babies.'

Robert looked embarrassed. 'Er . . . all right . . . er . . . thanks.'

And that, folks, was how Brody Miller got her life back.

Chapter Twenty-Seven

I almost bounced out of the car when Mom dropped me off at After School club. 'I'll just turn round and pick Jake up then be back for you in about half an hour, OK? See you soon, hon,' Mom called after me.

'Not if I see you first.'

Did I really just say that? I'd have to work on my repartee; I'd gotten rusty. I hurried through the gate, wanting to skip but holding back like the well-trained Hairy Mary I was. I had the feeling Mom was still in the car watching, so before I disappeared from view I turned and waved. I was right; she was still there, staring straight at me. I just knew she'd have a grin on her face. My mom—I just love that woman to bits. This weekend I'd be buying her the biggest bunch of flowers she'd ever had in her life to say thank you for getting me through this. Dad, too. Though maybe not flowers for him. What would he like? Oh, yes, perfect. I'd let him go back to work! The house was buzzing with security. Any burglar trying their luck on Kirkham Lodge from now on would need at least a masters degree in electronics. I felt as safe as anyone could.

I entered the mobile, whistling tunelessly, said 'Hi' to Mr Wesley as I signed myself in and immediately searched round for Reggie. I was worried I might have missed him—it was past five thirty and some kids had already been signed out. I couldn't wait to tell him everything about my showdown with Robert, but he was over in the corner in a conference with Mrs Fryston and Ruby. It looked quite intense; Ruby was shaking her head defiantly as Mrs Fryston, kneeling down to get proper eye contact, was talking in a low, firm voice.

'What's going on over there?' I asked Sammie, who was pressing lids down on to the plastic boxes of candy at the sweet stall.

'Oh, you've missed a right do,' Sammie whispered loudly, nodding as I offered to help put away the marshmallows. 'Ruby and Brandon got into one of their arguments over the cowboy boots. Brandon walked off to show he wasn't bothered so Ruby chucked the boot after him but it missed and hit Tasmim on the back of her head instead. The heel cut her and made it bleed; luckily she's got black hair so it didn't show much but Mrs McCormack used up nearly all the cotton wool in the first-aid box dabbing it up. You can see for yourself if you look in the bin.'

'Er . . . no thanks.'

'Tasmim's mum was not impressed about it when she arrived, I can tell you. She had a right go at Mrs Fryston and I reckon Mrs Fryston's going to have a right go at Mrs Glazzard when she comes.'

'Oh,' I said, glancing over, hoping to catch Reggie's eye to sympathize, but he was staring at his feet, looking real fed up. It struck me how unfair it was Reggie was always being dragged into things Ruby had done. He reminded me of Orla, having to be there to pick up the pieces every time.

'Anyway, how come you're so late?' Sammie asked, as direct as ever.

Boy, would she just love to know, but I wasn't ready to share this with the rest of the world yet, just Reggie Boy. 'Oh, I had to take part in a . . . debate,' I told her then switched subjects fast. 'How come you're putting away the sweet stall? I thought that was Sam territory?'

Sammie frowned. 'Oh, he hasn't done it for ages because of the book quiz so I'm in charge now.

I'll be glad when that thing's over and done with, I'm telling you. Sam's more stressed out over that quiz than his SATs, which is saying something.'

'Why?'

The final lid was pressed down with a thwack. 'Oh well, you know, after what happened in the last round.'

'What happened in the last round?' I asked.

She opened her mouth then closed it again, as if she'd just realized who she was telling. 'Best ask them,' she said, indicating Lloyd, Alex, and Sam over in the book zone, apparently doing some sort of drama piece. I looked but knew I couldn't just go over to them and start interfering again. They'd blanked me last time I'd asked and I couldn't risk being blanked again. I didn't want anything to burst my bubble just yet.

I sighed, looking round for something to do, when Mrs Glazzard arrived. Our eyes locked and she didn't exactly return my smile. I looked away quickly, not wanting her to think I was smiling because of the Ruby trouble ahead. 'Tell me,' I said to Sammie urgently, wanting to seem as if I had been engrossed in conversation. 'Tell me what happened during the last round.'

Sammie looked at me quizzically. 'Well, all right, as long as you don't tell them I told you or Sam'll stop talking to me.'

'Give me everything you got,' I told her as Ruby let out a wail.

And she did. Stupid, stupid me for asking.

Chapter Twenty-Eight

Why is life so complicated? I'd just had this big, life-changing experience in the café, right, not two hours ago. Two hours! You'd think Life or God or Karma or something would have eased up a little. 'Give the kid a break, guys, she's just come face-to-face with that burglar dude, she's got homework, she's got Reggie and his possessive mom and his flaky boot-throwing sister, she's got an appointment at the orthodontist's next week she doesn't even need. I repeat, give the kid a break—OK?' Nope. Not a chance. Straight from one drama to another.

'Don't even think about it,' I told myself as I went upstairs to get changed, 'what happened during Pick a Peck of Poets was not your fault.'

Half an hour later I was on the phone to Sam. He was in the middle of dinner—lamb and apricot stew, according to his mom—and sounded kind of surprised to hear from me. I launched straight in. 'Sam, is it true there was a complaint about me from that Tea-Time Tigers woman?'

'Erm . . .'

'She reckoned it was unfair I was in the team because I was much older than her guys and that gave us an unfair advantage, even though it was plain for everyone to see they didn't know squat?'

'Erm . . .'

'And Mrs Fryston said all points from the previous round were cancelled and everyone could start from scratch?'

'Erm . . .'

'And so, of course, that played straight into Tea-Time Tigers lady's hands because instead of that kid with the cast, she'd put this genius from the boys' school in her team, even though Alex found out he'd only ever been to an After School club once on an in-service day when he was six?'

'Erm . . . .'

'*And* the genius sat next to Lloyd and whispered mean things to him to put Lloyd off his stride?'

'Erm . . .'

'Why didn't you tell me? No, don't answer that. I know the answer to that. Sam, do you still need a fourth person for the team?'

'Erm . . . yes.'

'Will you do me a favour? Call the others and see if they want me back?'

'Are you serious?' he asked warily.

'Oh, I'm serious.'

'I don't need to call round, Brody. You know we do but only if you want to—no pressure.'

'Neat. You can go back to your dinner now.'

'Er . . . thanks.'

'By the way, I cannot disclose the source of this information.'

'Understood.'

Chapter Twenty-Nine

I'm going to move forward now to the next big thing that happened in my life. Sorry if that throws you out, guys, but come on, you don't want to hear all the boring details about me moving back into my original bedroom blah, blah, blah. Really, you don't. Any questions left over will be answered at the end, folks, I promise. This next bit is way more important. Trust me.

It is two weeks later: World Book Day. Picture the scene. We're in the Ad-Lib Room at Drury Lane Library in the centre of Wakefield. About forty kids, duly delivered by a stream of cars, minibuses, and taxis, are sitting cross-legged and over-awed in the elegant high-ceilinged function room, together with helpers, parents, librarians, and local press. Four teams (Crigglestone Kidz Out of Hours Club, Anston After Schoolers, ZAPS After School Club, and the Tea-Time Twerps) sit nervously waiting for the event to kick-off. Four judges (a children's librarian called Wendy, a VIP from the regional after-school club committee, a drama teacher, and the mayor—all high ranking honchos) sit behind a long, teak desk with questions at the ready. A very nervous Mrs Fryston stands at the front. A very smug looking After School club leader in a Simple Minds T-shirt stands at the back. A very hacked-off Brody Miller slides a note across to the genius from the boys' school called Charlie. The note reads: 'Bring it on.'

The final is a two-parter. For the first part, we have to 'interpret' an extract from one of the books in the 'Fantastic Classics' section. For the second part, we have to answer questions on the selected title. 'The questions will be a bit harder than last time,' Mrs Fryston had warned us.

Each team has to perform for a maximum of ten minutes and answer questions for five. We go in alphabetical order. That means we're last. Excellent.

Anston go first. They've chosen Mr Sharkey's favourite, *The Turbulent Term of Tyke Tyler.* They start off by cracking jokes, just like at the beginning of every chapter. Everyone laughs, including Brandon, the traitor! Then they act out a scene from the end of the book, where Tyke climbs the bell tower and everyone is shouting up at him. The kid playing Tyke gets carried away and falls off the chair. The audience is unsure whether it was intentional and therefore to clap or not or to call for an ambulance. Neat.

Crigglestone are up next. They do exactly the same as the first guys. Big mistake. The judges scribble away. 'They're writing the word "unoriginal",' I whisper to Lloyd. He looks back at me in hope. His face is as grey as an elephant's hide.

Then it's *them*. The Tea-Time Lily-Livered

Tigers. The Charlie kid makes a charlie out of himself. He may know every word of *The Secret Garden* inside out, upside down and in French, German, and Latin but he can't act. Worse still, nobody's had the guts to tell him. 'He should have played a tree,' I whisper to Lloyd. He looks at me and nods. He is still grey.

We're up. From beneath our tables, we dig out our costumes. The audience gasps when they see mine. Slowly, deliberately, I pull out the ankle-length white fake fur coat that caused such a stir when it was featured on the front cover of *ItGirl* in January and wrap it round me, holding it to my throat in a haughty manner. There are times when having a dad in the fashion industry really, really pays off. That and attending drama class at Hairy Mary's. Reggie wolf whistles but I ignore him.

Long Story Short. We are all awesome. At the end, Sam, as Edmund, delivers the icing on the cake. 'For you,' he says, politely, bowing in front of the judges and presenting Wendy the librarian with a box of Turkish Delight (if you haven't read the book, Turkish Delight plays a big part). Wendy smiles in . . . er . . . delight.

Round one to ZAPS. No fear.

Round two is trickier. The questions from the judges are much more probing. Forget the 'name the two main characters' lark. It's all 'in what way did the story affect you' kind of stuff. You get the feeling they're not looking for the answer, 'Dunno'. Charlie is spectacular on this round. His dad must be Philip Pullman or something. The judges are all nodding their heads far too enthusiastically, even Wendy, who now has icing sugar lips.

When it's our turn, we do OK, but there isn't as much of the enthusiastic head nodding Charlie got. The drama teacher asks us our final question. 'Don't you think the ending where Aslan comes back to life is a little unrealistic?' he asks. I look across at Sam, thinking he might like to field that one, but before he has a chance to speak, Lloyd is on his feet. Remember Lloyd, the shy, tongue-tied home-school kid with a grey face? Well, there must have been something in that Turkish Delight because everyone in that room now heard his clear, articulate and, it has to be said, slightly belligerent answer. Boy, did he let the drama teacher have it! Lloyd brought in re-incarnation, spirituality, symbolism, and the importance of helping children come to terms with death in a speech that had the judges open-mouthed and flicking through dictionaries.

'Where the heck did all that come from?' I asked Alex in amazement.

'Lloyd's grandad died at Christmas, remember.'

'Oh,' I said, not quite sure what she was getting at but then I didn't go to Sunday School like the pair of them did. Lloyd sat down again with a thud. The audience go wild.

It is with great delight (sorry, am I using that word too often?) I am able to tell you that Zetland Avenue Primary School After School Club won the Big Book Quiz. And they all lived happily ever after.

Epilogue

Do you want to know what I think? There are some things that can be fixed and some things that can't. My fear of burglars. Check. Making sure I get to school on time. Check. Making up to my friends and Mrs Fryston at After School club for letting them down in the book quiz by re-joining the team in time for the final and apologizing afterwards for my rudeness? Check. Being friends with Reggie again. Check. Having him back as my boyfriend. Double-check. Having his mom know and approve of that last item. *Nooooo*. Not yet. Not until the right time comes. That's what Reggie keeps telling me. Between you and me I don't think the right time is ever going to come. I think the day Mrs Glazzard saw me with Reggie in the shed was such a shock for her she'll never get over it. I don't take it personally; I just keep a low profile and avoid equipment sheds when I know she's around.

Besides, the poor woman has enough stress in her life. After the boot-throwing incident, Mrs Fryston suggested maybe Ruby wasn't ready to do a whole day at school and come to After School club on top, just yet. She generously put Ruby's behaviour down to tiredness. Mrs Glazzard didn't take to the recommendation too well, especially when her previous childminder refused to take Ruby back under 'any circumstances'. What does that tell you?

In the end, Mrs Glazzard had to cut her hours at work and pick Ruby up from school herself. Reggie says Ruby's been heaps better because she's getting the attention she needs but his mom is worn out! I'm thinking maybe if she gave Ruby a little more attention and Reggie a little less she'd have a quieter life but hey, I am not complaining. After School club is back to how it was, with Reggie a lot happier now he doesn't have to shield his cajones every time he enters the joint.

I'm a lot happier, too. I feel I belong again. I have learned not to jump every time Mrs Fryston needs a favour but I also know when I *should* help out. I'm Brody the Reliable and Brody the Hanging-back-a-Little. Two for the price of one. I still feel too old for the place sometimes, though, and Reggie's the same. I can't see me coming when I'm in Year Eight, to be honest. I'll definitely stick it out until the end of the year, though. No way am I going to miss Mrs Fryston's wedding to Mr Sharkey; that is going to be one neat event. I'm not as involved with the arrangements as Alex is, though, so I guess she's the one you need to check out next for details.

Bye, y'all,

Brody

PS: I've just thought of something important about the burglary issue. I know I got over my ordeal and did the whole face-to-face thing but there must be heaps of kids who have had a similar experience but for whom it doesn't end so good. Either the guy never gets caught or they turn out to be much nastier than Robert Voyle (who lives and works on his uncle's farm in Ireland now with Orla and a dog called Finbar). Anyway, one of the things Mom came across when she was trying to help me was this organization called *Victim Support*. The *Victim Supportline* number is **0845 3030900** and they have specialists who are trained to listen and offer guidance. It's just an idea if you're going through a hard time. Hope it helps.

The girls are back...

Sammie's Back

—the girl who makes a wish (but then really wishes she hadn't)

Helena Pielichaty

It wasn't my fault!

*All I did was try to bring everyone together again.
I just wanted it to be how it used to be—before dad left.
That's not so wrong, it is?*

*But as usual, it all went pear-shaped. Why does
everything I do turn into a complete nightmare?
I feel like such an idiot.*

*I bet everyone else's families are perfect. Well, they
would be, wouldn't they—their lives are all brilliant
compared to mine . . .*

ISBN-13: 978-0-19-275377-9
ISBN-10: 0-19-275377-0

What a nightmare!

*All I want is a quiet life—but do you think that's possible?
No chance.*

*It started off fine. With one best friend and out-of-school stuff
kept to almost zero, I had no worries. But then it all went
wrong. First there was the secret, then the secret about the
secret . . . and now everything's out of control!*

*The only time I feel calm is when I'm talking to my brother
Daniel—at least he never answers back. OK, so he's been
dead for years, but I don't have a problem with that—
unfortunately my family obviously does . . .*

ISBN-13: 978-0-19-275279-6
ISBN-10: 0-19-275279-7

It's crunch-time!

I'd been really looking forward to visiting Brody, Alex, and the rest of the gang—but now I'm not so sure I should have come at such a major time. My mum and stepdad, Darryl, aren't getting on. She's such an old nag—I don't know how Darryl puts up with her.

Well, if push comes to shove I know exactly where I want to be. And it's not with Mum, that's for sure. If she can divorce Darryl, then I'll divorce her—end of story! And until they sort it out I'm staying down here with my mates, even if it means doing another runner . . .

ISBN-13: 978-0-19-275380-9
ISBN-10: 0-19-275380-0

Helena Pielichaty (pronounced Pierre-li-hatty) was born in Stockholm, Sweden, but most of her childhood was spent in Yorkshire. Her English teacher wrote of her in Year Nine that she produced 'lively and quite sound work but she must be careful not to let the liveliness go too far.' Following this advice, Helena never took her liveliness further south than East Grinstead, where she began her career as a teacher. She didn't begin writing until she was 32. Since then, Helena has written many books for Oxford University Press. She lives in Nottinghamshire with her husband and two children.

www.helena-pielichaty.com